THE INCA EMERALD

From the heart of the jungle sounded the deep, coughing
roar of a jaguar

THE
INCA EMERALD

BY
SAMUEL SCOVILLE, Jr.
Author of "Boy Scouts in the Wilderness," "The
Blue Pearl," etc.

ILLUSTRATED BY
CHARLES LIVINGSTON BULL

NEW YORK
THE CENTURY CO.
1922

To

ALICE TRUMBULL SCOVILLE

My Kindest Critic

CONTENTS

LIST OF ILLUSTRATIONS

THE INCA EMERALD

THE INCA EMERALD

CHAPTER I

THE BEGINNING

IT was a bushmaster which started the
Quest of the Emerald—and only a possible bushmaster at that. One May evening in Cornwall, Big Jim Donegan, the lumber-king; sat in the misty moon-light with his
slippered feet on the rail of the veranda of
the great house in which he lived alone. He
was puffing away at a corn-cob pipe as
placidly as if he did not have more millions
than Cornwall has hills—which is saying
something, for Cornwall has twenty-seven
of the latter. Along the gravel walk, which
wound its way for nearly half a mile to the
entrance of the estate, came the sound of

a dragging footstep. A moment later, from out of the shadows stepped a man over six feet in height, a little stooped, and who wore a shiny frock-coat surmounted by a somewhat battered silk hat. The stranger had a long, clean-shaven, lantern-jawed face. His nose jutted out like a huge beak, a magnificent, domineering nose, which, however, did not seem in accord with his abstracted blue eyes and his precise voice.

"What do you want?" snapped Big Jim, bringing his feet to the floor with alarming suddenness.

The stranger blinked at him mildly for a moment with a gaze that seemed to be cataloguing the speaker.

"This is Mr. James Donegan," he finally stated.

"How do you know?" demanded the lumber-king.

"You have all the characteristics of a magnate," returned the other, calmly, "energy, confidence, bad temper, worse manners, and—"

"Whoa!" shouted Big Jim, whose bark was worse than his bite and who always respected people who stood up to him. "Never mind any more statistics. Who are you!"

"My name is Ditson," responded the other, sitting down without invitation in the most comfortable chair in sight. "Professor Amandus Ditson. I am connected with the Smithsonian National Museum."

"Well," returned Mr. Donegan, stiffening, "I don't intend to subscribe any money to the Smithsonian Museum or any other museum, so there's no use of your asking me."

"I had no intention of asking you for anything," returned Professor Ditson, severely. "I had understood that you were a collector of gems, and I came to place at your disposal certain information in regard to the finest emeralds probably now in existence. I too am a collector," he went on abstractedly.

"Humph!" grunted Big Jim. "What do

you collect?" he inquired, regarding his visitor shrewdly.

"Bushmasters," responded Professor Ditson, simply.

"Come again," returned Big Jim, much puzzled, "I don't quite get you. What are bushmasters?"

"The bushmaster," announced Professor Ditson, with more animation than he had yet shown, "is the largest, the rarest and the deadliest of South American serpents. It attains a length of over twelve feet and has fangs an inch and a half long. You will hardly believe me," he went on, tapping Mr. Donegan's knee with a long, bony forefinger, "but there is not a single living specimen in captivity at present, even in our largest cities."

The lumber-king regarded the scientist with undisguised astonishment.

"Professor Amandus Ditson," he announced solemnly, "so far as I 'm concerned, there can continue to be a lack of bushmasters not only in our great cities, but everywhere else.

"The bushmaster is the largest, rarest. and deadliest of
South American serpents"

Snakes of any kind are absolutely nothing in my young life."

"Tut! tut!" responded the professor, reprovingly. "I think that I could convince you that you are wrong in your unfortunate aversion to reptiles."

"No you could n't," returned Big Jim, positively, "not if you were to lecture all the rest of the year."

"Well," responded Professor Ditson soothingly, "suppose we discuss your hobby, which I understand is precious stones."

"Now you 're talking," returned the other, enthusiastically, "I suppose I 've about the finest collection of gems in this country, and in some lines perhaps the best on earth. Take pearls, for instance," he boasted. "Why, Professor Ditson, some boys right here in Cornwall helped me get the finest examples of pink and blue pearls that there are in any collection. When it comes to emeralds, there are half a dozen collectors who beat me out. What 's all this dope you have about them, anyway?"

"Last year," replied the other, "I was in Peru at a time when they were repairing one of the oldest cathedrals in that country. A native workman, knowing that I was interested in rarities of all kinds, brought me an old manuscript, which turned out to be a map and a description of the celebrated Lake of Eldorado."

"That's the name of one of those dream places," interrupted Mr. Donegan, impatiently. "I've no time to listen to dreams."

Professor Ditson was much incensed.

"Sir," he returned austerely, "I deal in facts, not in dreams. I have traveled one thousand miles to see you, but if you can not speak more civilly, I shall be compelled to terminate this interview and go to some one with better manners and more sense."

"Just what I was going to suggest," murmured Big Jim, taken aback, but much pleased by the professor's independence. "So long, however, as you've beat me to it, go on. I'll hear you out anyway."

Professor Ditson stared at him sternly.

"For nearly four hundred years," he began at last, "there have been legends of a sacred lake somewhere in Bolivia or Peru. Once a year, before the Spanish conquest, the chief of the Incas, the dominant race of Peru, covered with gold-dust, would be ferried out to the center of this lake. There he would throw into the lake the best emerald that had been found in their mines during the year and then leap in himself. At the same time the other members of the tribe would stand on the shores with their backs to the lake and throw into the water over their shoulders emeralds and gold ornaments."

"Why on earth did they do that?" exclaimed the old collector.

"As an offering to the Spirit of the Lake," returned the professor. "The Spaniards, when they heard the story, named the lake, Eldorado—The Lake of the Golden Man. As the centuries went by, the location was lost—until I found it again."

There was a long pause, which was broken at last by the lumber-king.

"Have you any proof that this story of yours is true?" he inquired sarcastically.

For answer, the scientist fished a dingy bag from his pocket and shook out on the table a circlet of soft, pale gold in which gleamed three green stones.

"I found this ten feet from the shore," he said simply.

The lumber-king gasped as he studied the stones with an expert eye.

"Professor Ditson," he admitted at last, "you're all right and I'm all wrong. That's South American gold. I know it by the color. African gold is the deepest, and South American the palest. Those stones are emeralds," he went on; "flawed ones, to be sure, but of the right color. The common emerald from the Ural Mountains is grass-green," lectured Mr. Donegan, fairly started on his hobby. "A few emeralds are gray-green. Those come from the old mines of the Pharaohs along the coast of the Red Sea. They are found on mummies and in the ruins of Pompeii and along the beach in front of Alexandria, where treasure-ships have been wrecked."

Professor Ditson yawned rudely.

"Once in a blue moon," went on the old collector, earnestly, "a real spring-green emerald with a velvety luster, like these stones, turns up. We call 'em 'treasure emeralds,' " he continued, while Professor Ditson shifted uneasily in his chair. Most of them are in Spanish collections, and they are supposed to be part of the loot that Cortez and Pizarro brought back to Spain when they conquered Mexico and Peru. How large did these old Peruvian emeralds run?" he inquired suddenly.

He had to repeat this question before Professor Ditson, who had been dozing lightly, roused himself.

"Ah yes, quite so, very interesting, I'm sure," responded that scientist, confusedly. "As to the size of South American emeralds," he went on, rubbing his eyes, "the Spanish record shows that Pizarro sent back to Spain several which were as large as pigeon eggs, and there is a native tradition that the last Inca threw into Eldorado an oval emerald as large as a hen's egg."

Donegan's face flushed with excitement.

"Professor Ditson," he said at last, "I 've got to have one of those emeralds. Come in," he went on, getting up suddenly, "and I 'll show you my collection."

Professor Ditson sat still.

"No, Mr. Donegan," he said, "it would be just a waste of time. To me, gems are just a lot of colored crystals."

The old lumber-king snorted.

"I suppose you prefer snakes," he said cuttingly.

Professor Ditson's face brightened at the word.

"There," he said enthusiastically, "is something worth while. I only wish that I had you in my snake-room. I could show you live, uncaged specimens which would interest you deeply."

"They sure would," returned Mr. Donegan, shivering slightly. "Well," he went on, "every man to his own taste. What 's your idea about this emerald secret? Can we do business together?"

The professor's face assumed an air of what he fondly believed to be great astuteness.

"I would suggest," he said, "that you fit out an expedition to the Amazon basin under my direction, to remain there until I collect one or more perfect specimens of the bushmaster. Then I will guide the party to Eldorado and assist them, as far as I can, to recover the sunken treasure."

He came to a full stop.

"Well," queried the lumber-king, "what else?"

The professor looked at him in surprise. "I have nothing else to suggest," he said.

"Suppose we get emeralds which may be worth hundreds of thousands of dollars—what percentage will you claim?" persisted Mr. Donegan.

"I thought that I had made it plain," returned the professor, impatiently, "that I have no interest whatever in emeralds. If you will pay the expenses of the expedition and allow me to keep as my own property any specimens of bushmasters obtained, it will be entirely satisfactory to me. Of course," finished the scientist, generously, "if we catch several bushmasters, I should have no objections to your having one."

"Heaven forbid!" returned the lumberking. "Professor," he went on with great emphasis, "I am perfectly willing that you shall have absolutely for your own use and benefit any and all bushmasters, crocodiles, snakes, toads, tarantulas, and any other similar bricà-brac which you may find in South America. Moreover," he continued, "I'll fit out an expedition right here from Cornwall that will do the business for both of us. There's a goodfor-nothin' old chap in this town named Jud Adams who has been all over the North huntin' an' trappin' an' prospectin'. In his younger days he was a pearl-diver. Then there're two young fellows here that went off last year with him for me and brought back the finest blue pearl in the world. I ain't got no manner of doubt but what all three of 'em will jump at the chance to go after emeralds and bushmasters."

"Bushmasters and emeralds, please," corrected the professor.

"Just as you say," responded the lumber-king. "Now you come right in and I'll put you up for the night and we'll send over at once for the crowd that I have in mind and get this expedition started right away."

"The sooner the better," responded the professor, heartily. "Any day, some collector may bring back a bushmaster and beat me out with the Smithsonian."

"I feel the same way," agreed the lumber-king. "I want Jim Donegan to have the first crack at those Inca emeralds."

While all this talk about gold and emeralds and bushmasters was going on in Big Jim's big house, over in a little house on the tiptop of Yelpin Hill, Jud Adams, the old trapper, was just sitting down to supper with two of his best friends. One of these was Will Bright, a magnificently built boy of eighteen with copper-colored hair and dark blue eyes,

and the other his chum, Joe Couteau, silent,
lithe, and swart as his Indian ancestors.
Jud himself was not much over five feet
tall, with bushy gray hair and beard and
steel-sharp eyes.   These three, with Fred Per-
kins, the runner, had won their way to Goreloi,
the Island of the Bear, and brought back Jim
Donegan's most prized gem, as already chronicled in "The Blue Pearl."   They had learned
to care for one another as only those can who
have fought together against monsters of the
sea, savage beasts, and more savage men.   Joe
and Will, moreover, had shared other life-and-
death adventures together, as told in "Boy
Scouts in the Wilderness," and, starting without clothes, food, or fire, had lived a month in
the heart of the woods, discovered the secret of
Wizard Pond, and broken up Scar Dawson's
gang of outlaws.   Will never forgot that Joe
had saved him from the carcajou, nor Joe that
it was Will who gave him the first chance of
safety when the bloodhounds were hot on their
heels through the hidden passage from Wizard
Pond.   Each one of the four, as his share of

the blue pearl, and the sea-otter pelt brought back from Akotan, had received fifteen thousand dollars. Fred had invested his money in his brother's business in Boston, left Cornwall, and bade fair to settle down into a successful business man. Will and Joe had both set aside from their share enough to take them through Yale. As for Jud, the day after he received his winnings in the game which the four had played against danger and death, he had a short interview with his old friend Mr. Donegan.

"All my life long," began Jud, "I 've been makin' money; but so far, I have n't got a cent saved up. I know how to tame 'most any other kind of wild animal, but money allers gets away from me. They do say, Jim," went on the old man, "that you 've got the knack of keepin' it. Probably you would n't be worth your salt out in the woods, but every man 's got somethin' that he can do better 'n most. So you just take my share of the blue-pearl money an' put it into somethin' safe an' sound that 'll bring me an income. You see, Jim," he went on confidentially, "I ain't so young as I used to be."

"I should say you ain't!" exclaimed Big Jim, knowing how Jud hated to be called old. "You 're 'most a hundred now."

"I ain't! I ain't!" howled Jud, indignantly. "I ain't a day over fifty—or thereabouts."

"Well, well," said his friend, soothingly, "we won't quarrel over it. I 'll take care of your money and see that you get all that 's comin' to you for the two or three years which you 've got left"; and with mutual abuse and affection the two parted as good friends as ever.

To-night the old trapper and his guests had just finished supper when the telephone rang.

"Jud," came Mr. Donegan's voice over the wire, "what would you and Bill and Joe think of another expedition—after emeralds this time?"

"We 'd think well of it," returned Jud,

promptly. "The kids are here at my house now."

"Good work!" exclaimed the lumber-king. "All three of you come right over. I've got a scientist here who's going to guide you to where the emeralds grow."

"You got a what?" queried Jud.

"A scientist!" shouted Big Jim, "a perfesser. One of those fellows who know all about everything except what's useful."

"We'll be right over," said Jud, hanging up the receiver and breaking the news to his friends.

"Listens good," said Will, while Joe grunted approvingly.

"It's a pity old Jim ain't young and supple enough to go on these trips with us himself," remarked Jud, complacently.

"He ten years younger than you," suggested Joe, slyly, who always delighted in teasing the old trapper about his age.

"Where do you get such stuff?" returned Jud, indignantly. "Jim Donegan's old enough to be my father—or my brother, anyway," he finished, staring sternly at his grinning guests.

"You 're quite right, Jud," said Will, soothingly. "Let's go, though, before that scientist chap gets away."

"He no get away," remarked Joe, sorrowfully, who had listened to the telephone conversation. "He go with us."

"I don't think much of that," said Jud, wagging his head solemnly. "The last perfesser I traveled with was while I was prospectin' down in Arizona. He sold a cure for snakebites an' small-pox, an' one night he lit out with all our cash an' we never did catch him."

Half an hour later found the whole party in Mr. Donegan's study, where they were introduced to Professor Ditson.

"What might you be a perfesser of?" inquired Jud, staring at him with unconcealed hostility.

The other stared back at him for a moment before he replied.

"I have specialized," he said at last, "in reptiles, mammals, and birds, besides some research work in botany."

"Did n't leave out much, did you?" sneered Jud.

"Also," went on the professor, more quietly, "I learned early in life something about politeness. You would find it an interesting study," he went on, turning away.

"Now, now," broke in Mr. Donegan, as Jud swallowed hard, "if you fellows are going treasure-hunting together, you must n't begin by scrappin'."

"I, sir," returned Professor Ditson, austerely, "have no intention of engaging in an altercation with any one. In the course of collecting-trips in the unsettled portions of all four continents, I have learned to live on good terms with vagabonds of all kinds, and I can do it again if necessary."

"Exactly!" broke in Mr. Donegan, hurriedly, before Jud could speak; "that certainly shows a friendly spirit, and I am sure Jud feels the same way."

"I do," returned the latter, puffingly, "just the same way. I got along once with a per-

fesser who was no darn good, and I guess I
can again."

"Then," said Mr. Donegan, briskly, "let's
get down to business. Professor Ditson, show
us, please, the map and manuscript with which
you located Lake Eldorado."

For reply, the gaunt scientist produced from
a pocket a small copper cylinder, from which
he drew a roll of yellowed parchment. Half
of it was covered with crabbed writing in the
imperishable sepia ink which the old scriv-
eners used. The other half was apparently
blank. The lumber-king screwed his face up
wisely over the writing.

"H'm-m," he remarked at last. "It's some
foreign language. Let one of these young
fellers who're going to college try."

Will took one look at the paper.

"I pass," he said simply; while Joe shook
his head without even looking.

"You're a fine lot of scholars!" scoffed Jud,
as he received the scroll. "Listen now to
Perfesser Adams of the University of Out-
of-Doors."

Then, to the astonishment of everybody, in his high-pitched voice he began to translate the labored lines, reading haltingly, like a school-boy:

"I, Alvarado, companion of Pizarro, about to die at dawn, to my dear wife Oriana. I do repent me of my many sins. I am he who slew the Inca Atahualpa and many of his people, and who played away the Sun before sunrise. Now it comes that I too must die, nor of the wealth that I have won have I aught save the Secret of Eldorado. On a night of the full moon, I myself saw the Golden Man throw into the lake the great Emerald of the Incas and a wealth of gold and gems. This treasure-lake lies not far from Orcos in which was thrown the Chain. I have drawn a map in the way thou didst show me long years ago. Take it to the king. There be treasure enough there for all Spain; and through his justice, thou and our children shall have a share. Forgive me, Oriana, and forget me not.

"ALVARADO"

There was a silence when he had finished.

It was as if the shadow of the tragedy of that wasted life and vain repentance had drifted down the centuries and hung over the little company who had listened to the reading of the undelivered letter. The stillness was broken by Mr. Donegan.

"Where did you learn to read Spanish, you old rascal?" he inquired of Jud.

"Down among the Greasers in Mexico," chuckled the latter, delightedly.

"What does he mean by 'playing away the Sun' and the 'Chain'?" asked Will, of the scientist.

"When the treasures of the Incas were divided," explained Professor Ditson, precisely, "Alvarado had for his share a golden image of the sun over ten feet in diameter. This he gambled away in a single night. The Chain," continued Professor Ditson, "surrounded the chief Inca's residence. It was made of gold, and was two hundred and thirty-three yards long. It was being carried by two hundred Indians to Cuzco to form part of the chief's ransom—a room filled with gold as high as he could reach. When the gold came to his shoulder, he was killed. At the news of his death, the men who were bringing the Chain threw it into Lake Orcos."

"But—but," broke in the lumber-king, "where is the map? If you've got it with you, let's have a look at it."

Without speaking, Professor Ditson reached over and took the match from the table. Lighting it, he held the flame for an instant close to the parchment. On the smooth surface before their eyes, suddenly appeared a series of vivid green lines, which at last took the form of a rude map.

"What he learned from Oriana," explained Profesor Ditson, "was how to make and use invisible ink."

"Fellows," broke in Mr. Donegan, earnestly, "I believe that Professor Ditson has found Eldorado, and I'm willing to go the limit to get one of the emeralds of the Incas. I'll finance the expedition if you'll all go. What do you say?"

"Aye," voted Will.

"Aye," grunted Joe.

"I assent," said Professor Ditson, with his usual preciseness.

Jud alone said nothing.

"How about it, Jud?" inquired Big Jim.

"Well," returned Jud, doubtfully, "who's goin' to lead this expedition?"

"Why, the professor here," returned the lumber-king, surprised. "He's the only one who knows the way."

"That's it," objected Jud. "It's likely to be a rough trip, an' treasure-huntin' is always dangerous. Has the perfesser enough pep to keep up with us younger men?"

Professor Diston smiled bleakly.

"I've been six times across South America, and once lived among the South American Indians for two years without seeing a white man," he remarked acidly. "Perhaps I can manage to keep up with an old man and two boys who have never been in the country before. You should understand," he went on, regarding the old trapper sternly, "that specialization in scientific investigation does not necessarily connote lack of physical ability."

Jud gasped. "I don't know what he means," he returned angrily, "but he's wrong—specially that part about me bein' old."

"I feel it is my duty to warn you," interrupted Professor Ditson, "that this trip may involve a special danger outside of those usual to the tropics. When I was last in Peru," he went on, "I had in my employ a man named Slaughter. He was an expert woodsman, but sinister in character and appearance and with great influence over the worst element among the Indians. One night I found him reading this manuscript, which he had taken from my tent while I was asleep. I persuaded him to give it up and leave my employ."

"How did you persuade him?" queried Jud, curiously.

"Automatically," responded Professor Ditson. "At least, I used a Colt's automatic," he explained. "His language, as he left, was deplorable," continued the scientist, "and he declared, among other things, that I would have him to reckon with if I ever went again to Eldorado. I have no doubt that through his Indian allies he will be advised of the expedition when it reaches Peru and make trouble for us."

"What did he look like?" inquired Mr. Donegan.

"He was a giant," replied Professor Ditson, "and must have been over seven feet in height. His eyebrows made a straight line across his forehead, and he had a scar from his right eye to the corner of his jaw."

"Scar Dawson!" shouted Will.

"You don't mean the one who nearly burned you and Joe alive in the cabin?" said the lumber-king, incredulously.

"It must be," said Will. "No other man would have that scar and height. "I'll say 'some danger' is right," he concluded, while Joe nodded his head somberly.

"That settles it!" said Jud. "It's evident this expedition needs a good man to keep these kids out of trouble. I'm on."

CHAPTER II

A NEW WORLD

A WEEK later found the whole party aboard of one of the great South American liners bound for Belem. The voyage across was uneventful except for the constant bickerings between Jud and Professor Ditson, in which Will and Joe acted sometimes as peace-makers and sometimes as pace-makers. Then, one morning, Will woke up to find that the ocean had changed overnight from a warm sap-green to a muddy clay-color. Although they were not within sight of land, the vast river had swept enough earth from the southern continent into the ocean to change the color of the water for a hundred miles out at sea. Just at sunrise the next day the steamer glided up the Amazon on its way to the old city of Belem, seventy miles inland.

"The air smells like a hot, mouldy cellar!"

grumbled Jud; and soon the Cornwall pilgrims began to glimpse things strange and new to all three of them. Groups of slim assai-palms showed their feathery foliage; slender lianas hung like green snakes from the trees; and everywhere were pineapple plants, bread-fruit trees, mangos, blossoming oranges and lemons, rows of enormous silk-cotton trees, and superb banana plants, with glossy, velvety green leaves twelve feet in length curving over the roof of nearly every house. Beyond the city the boys had a sight of the jungle, which almost without a break covers the greater part of the Amazon basin, the largest river-basin on earth. They landed just before sunset, and, under Professor Ditson's direction, a retinue of porters carried their luggage to the professor's house, far down the beach, the starting-point for many of his ·South American expeditions.

As the sun set, the sudden dark of the tropics dropped down upon them, with none of the twilight of higher latitudes. Jud grumbled at the novelty.

"This ain't no way to do," he complained

to Professor Ditson. "The sun no more than
goes down, when bang! it's as black as your
hat."

"We'll have that seen to at once," responded the professor, sarcastically. "In the
meantime, be as patient as you can."

With the coming of the dark, a deafening
din began. Frogs and toads croaked,
drummed, brayed, and roared. Locusts
whirred, and a vast variety of crickets and
grasshoppers added their shrill note to the up-
roar, so strange to visitors and so unnoticed by
natives in the tropics.

"Hey, Professor!" shouted Jud, above the
tumult, "what in time is all this noise, anyway?"

"What noise?" inquired Professor Ditson,
abstractedly.

The old trapper waved both hands in a
circle around his head and turned to the boys
for sympathy. "Sounds like the Cornwall
Drum and Fife Corps at its worst!" he
shrieked.

"What do you mean, Jud?" said Will, wink-
ing at Joe.

"Poor Jud!" chimed in the latter, shaking his head sadly, "this trip too much for him. He hearing noises inside his head."

For a moment, Jud looked so horrified that, in spite of their efforts to keep up the joke, the boys broke down and laughed uproariously.

"You 'll get so used to this," said Professor Ditson, at last understanding what they were talking about, "that after a few nights you won't notice it at all."

At the professor's bungalow they met two other members of the expedition. One of these was Hen Pine, a negro over six feet tall, but with shoulders of such width that he seemed much shorter. He had an enormous head that seemed to be set directly between his shoulders, so short and thick was his neck. Hen had been with Professor Ditson for many years, and, in spite of his size and strength, was of a happy, good-natured disposition, constantly showing his white teeth in irresistible smiles. Pinto, Professor Ditson's other retainer, was short and dark, an Indian of the Mundurucu tribe, that warlike people which early made an alliance of peace with the Portuguese pioneers of Brazil which they had always scrupulously kept. Pinto had an oval aquiline face, and his bare breast and arms had the cross-marks of dark-blue tattooing which showed him to have won high rank as a warrior on the lonely River of the Tapirs, where his tribe held their own against the fierce Mayas, those outlawed cannibals who are the terror of the South American forest.

That evening, after dinner, Professor Ditson took Jud and the boys out for a walk along the beach which stretched away in front of them in a long white curve under the light of the full moon. The night was full of strange sounds, and in the sky overhead burned new stars and unknown constellations, undimmed even by the moonlight, which showed like snow against the shadows of the jungle. Professor Ditson pointed out to the boys Agena and Bungula, a noble pair of first-magnitude stars never seen in the North, which flamed in the violet-black sky. As they looked, Will remembered the night up near Wizard Pond before the bear came, when Joe had told him Indian stories of the stars. To-night, almost overhead, shone the most famous of all tropical constellations, the Southern Cross.

Professor Ditson told them that it had been visible on the horizon of Jerusalem about the date of the Crucifixion. From that day, the precession of the equinoxes had carried it slowly southward, and it became unknown to Europeans until Amerigo Vespucci on his first voyage saw and exultantly wrote that he had seen the "Four Stars," of which the tradition had lingered. The professor told them that it was the sky-clock of the tropics and that sailors, shepherds, and other night-wanderers could tell the time within fifteen minutes of watch-time by the position of the two upper stars of this constellation.

"It looks more like a kite than a cross," interjected Jud. "What's that dark patch in the Milky Way?" he inquired, pointing to a strange black, blank space showing in the milky glimmer of the galaxy.

"That must be the Coal-sack," broke in

Will, before Professor Ditson could reply.

"I remember reading about it at school," he went on.

"When Magellan sailed around Cape Horn, his sailors saw it and were afraid that they would sail so far south that the sky would n't have any stars. What cheered them up," went on Will, "was the sight of old Orion, which stays in the sky in both hemispheres," and he pointed out the starry belt to Jud and Joe, with the sky-king Sirius shining above it instead of below as in the northern hemisphere.

As Jud and the boys stared up at the familiar line of the three stars, with rose-red Betelgeuse on one side and fire-white Rigel on the other, they too felt something of the same comfort that the old-time navigators had known at the sight of this constellation, steadfast even when the Great Bear and the Pole Star itself had faded from the sky. As they continued to gaze upward they caught sight of another star, which shone with a wild, blue gleam which rivaled the green glare of the dog-star, Sirius. Professor Ditson told them that it was Canopus, Mohammed's star, which he thought led him to victory, even as Napoleon believed that the planet Venus, seen by daylight, was his guiding star.   Then the professor traced for them that glittering river of stars, Eridanus, and showed them, guarding the southern horizon, gleaming Achernar, the End of the River, a star as bright as is Arcturus or Vega in the northern sky.   Then he showed them Fomalhaut, of the Southern Fish, which in the North they had seen in the fall just skipping the horizon, one of the faintest of the first-magnitude stars.   Down in the southern hemisphere it had come into its own and gleamed as brightly near this northern horizon as did Achernar by the southern.   It was Will who discovered the Magellanic Clouds, like fragments of the Milky Way which had broken up and floated down toward the South Pole.   These had been also seen and reported by Magellan on that first voyage ever taken around the world four hundred years ago.

Farther up the beach, Jud and the boys came to a full stop.   Before them towered so high that the stars seemed tangled in its leaves a royal palm, one of the most magnificent trees on earth. Its straight, tapered shaft shot up over a hundred and twenty-five feet and was crowned with a mass of glossy leaves, like deep-green plumes. As it touched the violet sky with the full moon rising back of its proud head, it had an air of unearthly majesty.

Beneath their feet the beach was covered with "angel-wings," pure white shells eight inches long, shaped like the wings of angels in old pictures. With them were beautifully tinted tellinas, crimson olivias with their wonderful zigzag, tentlike color patterns, large dosinias round as dollars, and many other varieties, gold, crimson, and purple.

Some distance down the beach the professor kept a large canoe, in which the whole party paddled out into the bay. As they flashed over the smooth surface, the clamor of the night-life dwindled. Suddenly, from the bushes on a little point, sounded a bird-song which held them all spellbound, a stream of joyous melody, full of rapid, ringing notes, yet with a purity of tone which made the song indescribably beautiful. It seemed to include the ethereal quality of the hermit-thrush, the lilt and richness of the thrasher, and the magic of the veery's song, and yet to be more beautiful than any or all of them together. On and on the magic melody flowed and rippled, throbbed and ebbed in the moonlight. Suddenly it stopped. Then from the same thicket burst out a medley of different songs. Some of them were slow and mellow. Others had silvery, bell-like trills. There were flutelike calls, gay hurried twitterings, and leisurely delicious strains—all of them songs of birds which the Cornwall visitors had never even heard. Then Will, the ornithologist of his party, began to hear songs which were familiar to him. There was the musical chuckle of the purple martin, the plaintive call of the upland plover, the curious "kow-kow" of the yellow-billed cuckoo, and the slow, labored music of the scarlet tanager. Suddenly all of them ceased and once again the original song burst out.

"That thicket must be chuck-full of birds," whispered Jud.

Professor Ditson shook his head.

"It's only one bird," he said, "but the greatest singer of all the world—the white banded mocking bird."

Even as he spoke, the songster itself fluttered up into the air, a brown bird with a white throat, and tail and wings broadly banded with the same color. Up and up it soared, and its notes chimed like a golden bell as its incomparable song drifted down through the moonlight to those listening below. Then on glistening wings the spent singer wavered down like some huge moth and disappeared in the dark of the thicket. In the silence that followed, Will drew a deep breath.

"I'd have traveled around the world to hear that song," he half whispered.

Professor Ditson nodded his head understandingly.

"Many and many an ornithologist," he said "has come to South America to listen to that bird and gone away without hearing what we have heard to-night. Between his own two songs," went on the professor, "I counted the notes of seventeen other birds of both North and South America that he mimicked."

They paddled gently toward the shore, hoping to hear the bird again, but it sang no more that night. As they neared the beach, the moonlit air was heavy with the scent of jessamine, fragrant only after darkness, and the overpowering perfume of night-blooming cereuses, whose satin-white blossoms were three feet in circumference. Suddenly, just before them, the moon-flowers bloomed. Great snowy blossoms five inches across began to open slowly. There was a puff of wind, and hundreds of them burst into bloom at once, glorious white salvers of beauty and fragrance.

"Everything here," said Will, "seems beautiful and peaceful and safe."

Professor Ditson smiled sardonically. "South America is beautiful," he said precisely, "but it is never safe. Death and danger lurk everywhere and in the most unexpected forms. It is only in South America," he went on, "that you can be eaten alive by fish the size of small trout, or be killed by ants or little brown bats."

Jud listened with much scorn. "Professor," he broke out at last, "I don't take much stock in that kind of talk. Your nerves are in a bad way. My advice to you is—"

What Mr. Judson Adams's advice was, will never be known, for at that moment a dreadful thing happened. Into the beauty of the moonlight, from the glassy water of the bay soared a shape of horror, a black, monstrous creature like a gigantic bat. It had two wings which measured a good twenty feet from tip to tip, and was flat, like an enormous skate. Behind it streamed a spiked, flexible tail, while long feelers, like slim horns, projected several feet beyond a vast hooked mouth. Like some vampire shape from the Pit, it skimmed through the air across the bow of the canoe not ten feet from where Jud was sitting. The old trapper was no coward, but this sudden horror was too much even for his seasoned nerves. With a yell, he fell backward off his thwart, and as his legs kicked con-

vulsively in the air, the monster came down
with a crash that could have been heard a
mile, raising a wave which nearly swamped
the canoe. A moment later, the monstrous
shape broke water again farther seaward,
blotting out for an instant with its black bulk
the rising moon.

"What kind of a sea-devil is that, any-
how?" queried Jud, shakily, as he righted
himself, with the second crash of the falling
body still in his ears.

"That," responded Professor Ditson, precisely, "is a well-nourished specimen of the
manta-ray, a fish allied to the skate family—
but you started to speak about nerves."

Jud, however, said nothing and kept on saying the same all the way back to the house.
Arriving there in safety, he went down to the
spring for some water with Pinto, but a moment later came bolting back.

"What's the matter now, Jud?" inquired
Will, solicitously. "Did you find another
water-devil in the spring?"

"That's just what I did!" bellowed Jud.

"When I started to dip out a pail of water, up pops about six feet of snake. Now you know, boys," he went on, panting, "I hate snakes, an' I jumped clear across the spring at the sight of this one; but what do you suppose that Injun did?" he continued excitedly. "Pats the snake's head an' tells me it's tame an' there to keep the spring free from frogs. Now what do you think of that?"

"He was quite right," observed Professor Ditson, soothingly. "It is a perfectly harmless, well-behaved serpent, known as the mussarama. This one is a fine specimen which it will be worth your while to examine more carefully."

"I've examined it just as carefully as I'm goin' to," shouted Jud, stamping into the house as Pinto came grunting up the path carrying a brimming bucket of water.

As they sat down for supper, a long streak of black and white flashed across the ceiling just over Jud, who sat staring at it with a spoonful of soup half-way to his mouth.

"Professor Ditson," he inquired softly, "is that thing on the ceiling another one of your tame snakes?"

"No, sir," responded the professor, impatiently; "that is only a harmless house-lizard."

"I just wanted to know," remarked Jud, rising and taking his plate to a bench outside of the door, where he finished his supper, in spite of all attempts on the part of the boys to bring him back.

In front of Will stood a pitcher of rich yellow cream. "You have a good cow, Professor Ditson," he remarked politely as he poured some into a cup of the delicious coffee which is served with every meal in Brazil.

"Yes," agreed the scientist, "I have a grove of them." Then he explained to the bewildered Will that the cream was the sap of the cow tree.

Will was not so fortunate with his next investigation. Taking a second helping of a good-tasting stew which Pinto had brought in from the kitchen, he asked the Indian what it was made of.

"Tinnala," replied the Mundurucu.

"What is it in North American?" persisted Will.

The Indian shook his head. "I not know any other name," he said. "Wait, I show you," he went on, disappearing into the kitchen to return a moment later with a long, hairy arm ending in a clenched fist. Will started up and clasped his stomach frantically, remembering all that he had read about cannibalism among the South American Indians. Even when Professor Ditson explained that the stew was made from a variety of monkey which was considered a great delicacy, he was not entirely reassured and finished his meal on oranges.

Jud was much amused. "You always were a fussy eater, Bill," he remarked from the porch. "I remember you would n't eat mountain-lion meat up in the North when we were after the pearl. You ought to pattern after Joe. He don't find fault with his food."

"All I want about food," grunted Joe, "is enough."

That night the whole party slept side by side in hammocks swung in a screened veranda in the second story.

During the night, Jud, who was always a light sleeper, was awakened by a curious, rustling, crackling sound which seemed to come from the storeroom, which opened into the sleeping-porch. After listening awhile he reached over and aroused Professor Ditson, who was sleeping soundly next to him.

"Some one 's stealin' your grub," he whispered.

The professor stepped lightly out of his hammock, followed by Jud and the boys, who had been waked up by the whispering. Opening the door noiselessly, the scientist peered in. After a long look, Professor Ditson turned around to find Jud gripping his revolver and ready for the worst.

"You can put up your gun," the scientist growled. "Bullets don't mean anything to thieves like these, and he flashed a light on a strange sight. On a long table stood native baskets full of cassava, that curious grainlike

substance obtained from the root of the poisonous manihot and which takes the place of
wheat in South America. The floor was
covered with moving columns of ants, large
and small, which had streamed up the legs of
the table and into the baskets. Some of them
were over an inch long, while others were
smaller than the grains they were carrying.
The noise which had aroused Jud had been
made by their cutting off the dry leaves with
which the baskets were lined, to use in lining
their underground nest. Professor ·Ditson
told them that nothing could stop an ant-army.
Once on the march, they would not turn back
for fire or water and would furiously attack
anything that tried to check them. "A re-
markably efficient insect," concluded the professor, "for it bites with one end and stings
with the other."

"This is what I call a nice quiet night!"
murmured Jud, as he went back to his hammock. "Sea-devils, snakes, lizards—and now
it's ants. I wonder what next?"

"Next," however, was daylight, blazing
with the startling suddenness of the tropics,

where there is no dawn-light. With the light,
the tumult of the night ceased, and in place
of the insect din came a medley of bird-notes.
When Jud opened his eyes Professor Ditson's
hammock was empty, for the scientist usually
got up long before daylight, and through the
open door strutted a long-legged, wide-winged
bird, nearly three feet tall, with a shimmering
blue breast and throat. Without hesitating,
she walked over to Jud's hammock and,
spread her wings with a deep murmuring
note, made a low bow.

"Good morning to you," responded Jud,
much pleased with his visitor.

The bird bowed and murmured again and
allowed him to pat her beautiful head as
she bent forward. Then she went to the next
hammock and the next and the next, until she
had awakened all of the sleepers, whereupon,
with deep bows and courtesies and murmur-
ings, she sidled out of the room.

"Now, that," said Jud, as he rolled out of
the hammock and began to look for his shoes,
"is an alarm-clock worth having!"

Pinto, the Mundurucu, who appeared at

this moment with a pail of spring water, told them that the bird was a tame female trumpeter which he had picked up as a queer, frightened little creature, all legs and neck, but which had become one of the best-loved of all of his many pets. Each morning the tame, beautiful bird would wander through the house, waking up every sleeper at sunrise. When Pinto took trips through the forest the bird always went with him, traveling on his back in a large-meshed fiber bag; and when he made camp it would parade around for a while, bowing and talking, and then fly up into the nearest tree, where it would spend the night. Tente, as it was named, was always gentle except when it met a dog. No matter how large or fierce the latter might be, Tente would fly at it, making a loud, rumbling noise, which always made the dog turn tail and run for its life.

As Pinto started to fill the pitchers, Will, the bird expert of the party, began to ask him about some of the songs which were sounding all around the house. One bird which squalled and mewed interested him.

"That bird chestnut cuckoo," said Pinto. "It have the soul of a cat."

And as Will listened he could well believe it. A little farther off, another bird called constantly, "Crispen, Crispen, Crispen."

"One time," narrated the Indian, "a girl and her little brother Crispen go walking in the woods. He very little boy and he wander away and get lost, and all day and all night and all next day she go through the woods calling, 'Crispen! Crispen! Crispen!' until at last she changed into a little bird. And still she flies through the woods and calls 'Crispen!' "

At this point, Jud finally found his missing shoes and started to put one on, but stopped at a shout from the Mundurucu.

"Shake it out!" warned Pinto. "No one ever puts on shoes in this country without shaking out."

Jud did as he was told. With the first shoe he drew a blank. Out of the second one, however, rattled down on the floor a centipede fully six inches long, which Pinto skillfully crushed with the heavy water-pitcher.

Jud gasped and sank back into his hammock.

"Boys," he said solemnly, "I doubt if I last out this trip!"

CHAPTER III

THE VAMPIRES

AFTER breakfast, Professor Amandus Ditson called the party together for a conference in a wide, cool veranda on the ground floor.

"I should like to outline to you my plan of our expedition," he announced precisely.

Jud gave an angry grunt. The old adventurer, who had been a hero among prospectors and trappers in the Far North, was accustomed to be consulted in any expedition of which he was a member.

"It seems to me, Professor Ditson," he remarked aggressively, "that you 're pretty uppity about this trip. Other people here have had experience in treasure-huntin'."

"Meaning yourself, I presume," returned Professor Ditson, acidly.

"Yes, sir!" shouted Jud, thoroughly aroused,

"that's exactly who I do mean. I know as much about—*ouch!*" The last exclamation came when Jud brought down his open hand for emphasis on the side of his chair and incidently on a lurid brown insect nearly three inches in length, with enormous nippers and a rounded body ending in what looked like a long sting. Jud jerked his hand away and gazed in horror at his threatening seat-mate.

"I believe I'm stung," he murmured faintly, gazing anziously at his hand. "What is it?"

"It would hardly seem to me," observed Professor Ditson, scathingly, "that a man who is afraid of a harmless arachnid like a whip-scorpion, and who nearly falls out of a canoe at the sight of a manta-ray disporting itself, would be the one to lead an expedition through the unexplored wilds of South America. We are going into a country," he went on more earnestly, "where a hasty step, the careless touching of a tree, or the tasting of a leaf or fruit may mean instant death, to say nothing of the dangers from some of the larger carnivora and wandering cannibals. I have had some experience with this region," he went on, "and if there is no objection, I will outline my plan."

There was none. Even Jud, who had removed himself to another chair with great rapidity, had not a word to say.

"I propose that we take a steamer by the end of this week to Manaos, a thousand miles up the Amazon," continued the professor. "In the meantime, we can do some hunting and collecting in this neighborhood. After we reach Manaos we can go by boat down the Rio Negros until we strike the old Slave Trail which leads across the Amazon basin and up into the highlands of Peru."

"Who made that trail?" inquired Will, much interested.

"It was cut by the Spanish conquerors of Peru nearly four hundred years ago," returned the scientist. "They used to send expeditions down into the Amazon region after slaves to work their mines. Since then," he went on, "it has been kept open by the Indians themselves, and, as far as I know, has not been traversed by a white man for centuries. I learned the secret of it many years ago, while I was living with one of the wilder tribes," he finished.

The professor's plan was adopted unanimously, Jud not voting.

Then followed nearly a week of wonderful hunting and collecting. Even Jud, who regarded everything with a severe and jaundiced eye, could not conceal his interest in the multitude of wonderful new sights, sounds, and scents which they experienced every day. As for Will, he lived in the delightful excitement which only a bird-student knows who finds himself surrounded by a host of unknown and beautiful birds. Some of them, unlike good children, were heard but not seen. Once, as they pushed their way in single file along a little path which wound through the jungle, there suddenly sounded, from the dark depths beyond, a shriek of agony and despair. In a moment it was taken up by another voice and another and another, until there were at least twenty screamers performing in chorus.

"It's only the ypicaha rail," remarked the professor, indifferently.

Hen Pine, who was in the rear with Will, shook his head doubtfully.

"Dis ol' jungle," he whispered, "is full o' squallers.   De professor he call 'em birds, but dey sound more like ha'nts to me."

Beyond the rail colony they heard at intervals a hollow, mysterious cry.

"That," explained Pinto, "is the Witch of the Woods.   No one ever sees her unless she is answered.   Then she comes and drives mad the one who called her."

"Nice cheery place, this!" broke in Jud.

"The alleged witch," remarked Professor Ditson severely, "happens to be the little waterhen."

Later they heard a strange, clanging noise, which sounded as if some one had struck a tree with an iron bar, and at intervals from the deepest part of the forest there came a single, wild, fierce cry. Even Professor Ditson could not identify these sounds.

"Dem most suttinly is ha'nts," volunteered Hen.   "I know 'em.   You would n't catch dis chile goin' far alone in dese woods."

One of the smaller birds which interested Will was the many-colored knight, which looked much like one of the northern kinglets. His little body, smaller than that of a house-wren, showed seven colors—black, white, green, blue, orange, yellow, and scarlet, and he had a blue crown and a sky-blue eye. Moreover, his nest, fastened to a single rush, was a marvel of skill and beauty, being made entirely of soft bits of dry, yellow sedge, cemented together with gum so smoothly that it looked as if it had been cast in a mold. Then there was the Bienteveo tyrant, a bird about nine inches long, which caught fish, flies, and game, and fed on fruit and carrion indiscriminately. It was entirely devoted to its mate, and whenever a pair of tyrants were separated, they would constantly call back and forth to each other reassuringly, even when they were hunting. When they finally met again, they would perch close to each other and scream joyously at being reunited. Another bird of the same family, the scarlet tyrant, all black and scarlet, was so brilliant that

even the rainbow-hued tanagers seemed pale
and the jeweled humming-bird sad-colored in
the presence of "coal-o'-fire," as the Indians
have named this bird.

Jud was more impressed with the wonders
of the vegetable kingdom. Whenever he
strayed off the beaten path or tried to cut his
way through a thicket, he tangled himself in
the curved spines of the pull-and-haul-back
vine, a thorny shrub which lives up to its name,
or was stabbed by the devil-plant, a sprawling
cactus which tries quite successfully to fill up
all the vacant spaces in the jungle where it
grows.   Each stem of this well-named shrub
had three or four angles, and each angle was
lined with thorns an inch or more in length,
so sharp and strong that they pierced Jud's
heavy hunting-boots like steel needles.   If it
had not been for Hen, who was a master with
the machete, Jud never would have broken
loose from his entanglements. Beyond the cactus, the old trapper came to a patch of poor-
man's plaster, a shrub with attractive yellow
flowers, but whose leaves, which broke off at
a touch, were covered on the under side with

barbed hairs, which caught and clung to any
one touching them. The farther Jud went, the
more he became plastered with these sticky
leaves, until he began to look like some huge
chrysalis. The end came when he tripped on
a network of invisible wires, the stems of
species of smilax and morning-glory, and
rolled over and over in a thicket of the plas-
ters. When at last he gained his feet, he
looked like nothing human, but seemed only
a walking mass of green leaves and clinging
stems.

"Yah, yah, yah!" roared Hen. "Mars' Jud
he look des like Br'er Rabbit did when he
spilled Br'er Bear's bucket o' honey over his-
self an' rolled in leafs tryin' to clean his-
self. Mars' Jud sure look like de grand-daddy
ob all de ha'nts in dese yere woods."

"Shut up, you fool darky," said Jud, de-
cidedly miffed. "Come and help unwrap me.
I feel like a cigar."

Hen laughed so that it was with difficulty
that he freed Jud, prancing with impatience,
from his many layers of leaves. Later on,
Hen showed himself to be an even more pres-

ent help in trouble. The two were following
a path a short distance away from the rest of
the party, with Jud in the lead. Suddenly
the trapper heard the slash of the negro's
machete just behind him, and turned around
to see him cutting the head from a coiled rattlesnake over which Jud had stepped. If
Jud had stopped or touched the snake with
either foot, he would most certainly have been
bitten, and it spoke well for Hen's presence of
mind that he kept perfectly quiet until the
danger was over. This South American rattlesnake had a smaller head and rougher scales
than any of the thirteen North American varieties, and was nearly six feet in length. Professor Ditson was filled with regret that it
had not been caught alive.

"Never kill a harmless snake," he said severely to Hen, "without consulting me. I
would have been glad to have added this specimen to the collection of the Zoölogical Gardens."

"Harmless!" yelled Jud, much incensed.
"A rattlesnake harmless! How do you get
that way?"

"He did n't do you any harm, did he?" retorted the professor, acidly. "It is certainly ungrateful of you to slander a snake just after he has saved your life."

"How did he save my life?" asked Jud.

"By not biting you," returned Professor Ditson, promptly.

A little later poor Jud had a hair-raising experience with another snake. He had shot a carancha, that curious South American hawk which wails and whines when it is happy, and, although a fruit-eater with weak claws and only a slightly hooked beak, attacks horses and kills lambs. Jud had tucked his specimen into a back pocket of his shooting-jacket and was following a little path which led through an open space in the jungle. He had turned over his shot-gun to Joe, and was trying his best to keep clear of any more tangling vines, when suddenly right beside him a great dark snake reared its head until its black glittering eyes looked level into Jud's, and its flickering tongue was not a foot from his face. With a yell, Jud broke the world's record for the back-standing broad-jump and tore down the trail shouting, "Bush-master! bushmaster!" at the top of his voice. As he ran he suddenly felt a sharp pain in his back.

"He's got me!" he called back to Hen Pine, who came hurrying after him. "Ouch! There he goes again!" and he plunged head-long into a patch of pull-and-haul-back vine, which anchored him until Hen came up.

"Dat ain't no bushmaster, Mars' Jud," the latter called soothingly. "Dat was only a trail-haunting blacksnake. He like to lie next to a path an' stick up his ol' head to see who's comin', kin' o' friendly like."

"Friendly nothin'!" groaned Jud. "He's just bit me again."

As soon as Hen laid hold of Jud's jacket he found out what was the matter. The hawk had only been stunned by Jud's shot and, com-ing to life again, had promptly sunk his claws into the latter's back, and Jud had mistaken the bird's talons for the fangs of the bush-master. Professor Ditson, who had hurried up, was much disappointed.

"If you ever meet a bushmaster, you'll learn the difference between it and a harmless blacksnake," he observed. "Probably, however," he went on thoughtfully, "it will be too late to do you much good."

"Why do all the snakes in South America pick on me?" complained Jud. "There don't seem to be nothin' here but snakes an' thorns."

It was Pinto who gave the old trapper his first favorable impression of the jungle. They had reached a deserted bungalow in the heart of the woods, which Professor Ditson had once made his headquarters a number of years before. There they planned to have lunch and spend the night. At the meal Jud showed his usual good appetite in spite of his misfortunes, but he complained afterward to Hen, who had attached himself specially to the old man, about the absence of dessert.

"I got a kind of a sweet tooth," he said. "You ain't got a piece of pie handy, have you?"

"No sah, no sah," replied Hen, regretfully. "You 's about three thousand miles south ob de pie-belt."

"Wait," broke in Pinto, who had been listening. "Wait a minute; I get you something sweet," and he led the way to an enormous tree with reddish, ragged bark. Some distance up its trunk was a deep hollow, out of which showed a spout of dark wax nearly two feet long. In and out of this buzzed a cloud of bees.

"I get you!" shouted Jud, much delighted, "a bee-tree! Look out, boy," he went on, as the Indian, clinging to the ridges of the bark with his fingers and toes, began to climb. "Those bees 'll sting you to death."

"South American bees hab no sting," explained Hen, as Pinto reached the wax spout, and, breaking it off, thrust his hand fearlessly through the cloud of bees into the store of honey beyond. A moment later, and he was back again, laden with masses of dripping honeycomb, the cells of which, instead of being six-sided, as with our northern bees, resembled each one a little bottle. The honey was clear and sweet, yet had a curious tart flavor. While Jud was sampling a bit of honeycomb, Pinto borrowed Hen's machete and cut a deep gash through the rough red bark of the tree. Immediately there flowed out from the cut the same thick, milky juice which they had seen at their first breakfast in South America. The Indian cut a separate gash for each one of the party, and they all finished their meal with draughts of the sweet, creamy juice.

"It sure is a land flowing with milk an' honey," remarked Jud, at last, after he had eaten and drunk all that he could hold.

"This vegetable milk is particularly rich in gluten," observed Professor Ditson, learnedly.

"I guess it'd gluten up a fellow's stomach all right if he drank too much of it," remarked Jud, smacking his lips over the sweet, sticky taste which the juice of the cow-tree left in his mouth.

After lunch, most of the party retired to their hammocks in the cool dark of the house for the siesta which South American travelers find an indispensable part of a tropical day. Only the scientist and Will stayed awake to catch butterflies through the scented silence of the forest where the air, filled with the steam and perfume of a green blaze of growth, had the wet hotness of a conservatory. When even the insects and the untiring tree-toads were silenced by the sun, Professor Ditson, wearing a gray linen suit with a low collar and a black tie, was as enthusiastic as ever over the collecting of rare specimens, and was greatly pleased at Will's interest in his out-of-door hobbies.

Together they stepped into the jungle, where scarlet passion-flowers shone like stars through the green. Almost immediately they began to see butterflies. The first one was a magnificent grass-green specimen, closely followed by others whose iridescent, mother-of-pearl wings gleamed in the sunlight like bits of rainbow. On a patch of damp sand a group made a cloud of sulphur-yellow, sapphire-blue, and gilded green-and-orange. The professor told Will that in other years he had found over seven hundred different kinds within an hour's walk from this forest bunga-low, being more than double the number of varieties found in all Europe.

Deep in the jungle, they at last came to a little open stretch where the Professor had often collected before and which to-day seemed full of butterflies. Never had Will imagined such a riot of color and beauty as there dazzled his eyes. Some of the butter-flies were red and yellow, the colors of Spain. Others were green, purple, and blue, bordered and spangled with spots of silver and gold. Then there were the strange transparent "glass-wings." One of these, the *Hetaira esmeralda,* Will was convinced must be the most beautiful of all flying creatures. Its wings were like clear glass, with a spot of mingled violet and rose in the center of each one. At a distance, only this shimmering spot could be seen rising and falling through the air, like the wind-borne petals of some beauti-ful flower. Indeed, as the procession of color drifted by, it seemed to the boy as if all the loveliest flowers on earth had taken to them-selves wings, or that the rainbow-bridge of the sky had been shattered into fragments which were drifting slowly down to earth.

The largest of them all were the swallow-tails, belonging to the same family as the tiger, and blue and black swallowtail, which Will had so often caught in Cornwall. One of that family gleamed in the sunlight like a blue meteor as it flapped its great wings, seven inches from tip to tip and of a dazzling blue, high above the tree-tops. Another member of the same family, and nearly as large, was satiny white in color. Professor Ditson told Will that both of these varieties were almost unknown in any collection, as they never came within twenty feet of the ground, so that the only specimens secured were those of disabled or imperfect butterflies which had dropped to the lower levels.

"Why could n't I climb to the top of one of those trees with a net and catch some?" inquired Will, looking wistfully up at the gleaming shapes flitting through the air so far above him.

"Fire-ants and wasps," returned the professor, concisely. "They are found in virtually every tree. No one can stand the pain of an ant's bite, and one sting of a Maribundi wasp has been known to kill a strong man."

That night, tired out by their long day of hunting, the whole party went to bed early. Will's sleeping-room was an upper screened alcove, just large enough to hold a single hammock. Somehow, even after his long hard day, he did not feel sleepy. Great trees shadowed his corner, so thick that even the stars could not shine through their leaves, and it seemed to Will as if he could stretch out his hands and lift up dripping masses of blackness, smothering, terrifying in its denseness. From a far-away tree-top the witch-owl muttered over and over again that mysterious word of evil, "Murucututu, murucututu," in a forgotten Indian tongue. He had laughed when Pinto told him a few nights before that the owl was trying to lay a spell on those who listened, but to-night in the dark he did not laugh.

Then close at hand in a neighborhood tree-top sounded a beautiful contralto frog-note slowly repeated. "Gul, gul, gul, gul, guggle, gul, guggle," it throbbed. The slow, sweet call gave the boy a sense of companionship, and he fell asleep with the music of it still sounding in his ears.

Toward midnight he woke with a vague sense of uneasiness. It was as if some hidden subconsciousness of danger had sounded an alarm note within his nerve centers and awakened him. Something seemed to be moving and whispering outside of the screened alcove. Then a body struck the screen of mosquito-netting, and he heard the rotten fiber rip. Another second, and his little room was filled with moving, flitting, invisible shapes. Great wings fanned the air just above his face. There was the faint reek of hot, furry bodies passing back and forth and all around him. For a moment Will lay thinking that he was in a nightmare, for he had that strange sense of horror which paralyzes one's muscles during a bad dream so that movement is impossible. At last, by a sudden effort, he stretched out his hand and struck a match from a box which stood on a stand beside his hammock. At the quick spurt of flame through the dark, from all parts of the little room came tiny, shrill screeches, and the air around him was black with whirling, darting shapes. Suddenly into the little circle of light from the match swept the horrible figure of a giant bat, whose leathern wings had a spread of nearly two and a half feet, and whose horrible face hovered and hung close to his own. Never had the boy believed that any created thing could be so grotesquely hideous. The face that peered into his own was flanked on each side by an enormous leathery ear. From the tip of the hairy muzzle grew a spearlike spike, and the grinning mouth was filled with rows of irregular, tiny, gleaming sharp teeth, gritting and clicking against each other. Deep-set little green eyes, which glistened and gleamed like glass, glared into Will's face. Before he could move, a great cloud of flying bats, large and small, settled down upon him. Some of them were small gray vampire-bats with white markings, others were the great fruit-eating bats, and there were still others dark-red, tawny-brown, and fox-yellow. Whirling and wheeling around the little point of flame, they dashed it out, and crawled all over the boy until he felt stifled and smothered with the heat of their clinging bodies.

Suddenly he felt a stinging pain in his bare shoulder and in one of his exposed feet. As he threw out his hands desperately, tiny clicking teeth cut the flesh of wrists and arms. The scent of blood seemed to madden the whole company of these deaths-in-the-dark, and, although the actual bites were made by the little vampire-bats, yet at the sight of them feasting, the other night-fliers descended upon the boy like a black cloud and clustered around the little wounds, as Will had seen moths gather around syrup spread on trees of a warm June night.

The sting of their bites lasted for only a second, and the flapping of their wings made a cool current of air which seemed to drug his senses. Dreamily he felt them against him, knew that they were draining his life, yet lacked the will-power to drive them away.

Suddenly there flashed into his mind all that he had heard and read of the deadly methods of these dark enemies of mankind. With a shriek, he threw out his arms through the furry cloud that hung over him and sprang out of his hammock.

At his scream, Professor Ditson rushed in with a flash-light, followed by Pinto, Hen, and Joe, while Jud slept serenely through the whole tumult. They found Will dripping with blood from a dozen little punctures made by the sharp teeth of the bats, and almost exhausted from fright and the loss of blood. Then came pandemonium. Seizing sticks, brooms, machetes, anything that came to hand, while Will sank back into his hammock, the others attacked the bats. Lighted by the flash of Professor Ditson's electric light, they drove the squeaking, shrieking cloud of dark figures back and forth through the little room until the last one had escaped through the torn netting or was lying dead on the floor.

Twenty-seven bats altogether were piled in a heap when the fight was over.

CHAPTER IV

DEATH RIVER

AT last their first week in this new world of beauty and mystery came to an end. At Belem they boarded a well-appointed steamer and embarked for the thousand-mile voyage to Manaos, which is only six degrees from the equator and one of the hottest cities of the world. There followed another week of a life that was strange and new to the travelers from Cornwall. There were silent, steaming days when the earth seemed to swoon beneath the glare of the lurid sun, and only at night would a breath of air cross the water, which gleamed like a silver burning-glass. For their very lives' sake, white men and Indians alike had learned to keep as quiet and cool as possible during those fiery hours. Only Hen, coming from a race that since the birth of time had lived close to the equator,

moved about with a cheerfulness which no
amount of heat or humidity could lessen. At
night, when the fatal sun had reluctantly disappeared in a mass of pink and violet clouds,
the life-bringing breeze would blow in fresh
and salt from the far-away sea, and all living
creatures would revive. The boys soon
learned that, in the mid-heat of a tropical sum-
mer, the night was the appointed time for
play and work, and they slept during the day
as much as possible in shaded, airy hammocks.

One evening, after an unusually trying day,
the night wind sprang up even before the sun
had set. Here and there, across the surface
of the river, flashed snow-white swallows with
dark wings. As the fire-gold of the sun
touched the horizon, the silver circle of the
full moon showed in the east, and for a moment the two great lights faced each other.
Then the sun slipped behind the rim of the
world, and the moon rose higher and higher,
while the Indian crew struck up a wailing
chant full of endless verses, with a strange
minor cadence like the folk-songs of the

Southern negro. Hen Pine translated the words of some of them, and crooned the wailing melody:

> "The moon is rising,
>   Mother, Mother,
> The seven stars are weeping,
>   Mother, Mother,
> To find themselves forsaken,
>   Mother, Mother."

Down the echoing channels, through the endless gloomy forests, the cadence of the song rose and fell.

Suddenly, in the still moonlight from the river-bank came a single low note of ethereal beauty and unutterable sorrow. Slowly it rose and swelled, keeping its heartbreaking quality and exquisite beauty. At the sound the men stopped singing, and it seemed as if an angel were sobbing in the stillness. On and on the song went, running through eight lonely, lovely notes which rose and swelled until there seemed to be nothing in the world except that beautiful voice, finally ending in a sob which brought the tears to Will's eyes.

Then out into the moonlight flitted the singer,
a quiet-colored little brown-and-gray bird, the
celebrated solitaire, the sweetest, saddest
singer of the Brazilian forest.

After all this music, supper was served. It
began with a thick, violet-colored drink in
long glasses filled with cracked ice. The boys
learned from Professor Ditson that this was
made from the fruit of the assai-palm. It was
strangely compounded of sweet and sour and
had besides a fragrance and a tingle which
made it indescribably refreshing. This was
followed by an iced preparation made from
the root of the manioc, whose juice is poisonous, but whose pulp is wholesome and delicious. Before being served it had been boiled
with the fruit of the miriti-palm, which added
a tart sweetness to its taste which the Northerners found most delightful. The next
course was a golden-yellow compound of a
rich, nutty flavor, the fruit of the mucuju-
palm, which has a yellow, fibrous pulp so full
of fat that vultures, dogs, and cats eat it greed-
ily. For dessert, there was a great basket of

sweet lemons, mangos, oranges, custard-apples, and other fruits.

After supper they all grouped themselves in the bow and there, in comfortable steamer-chairs, watched the steamer plow its way through a river of ink and silver. That day, Jud, while in his hammock, had seen, to his horror, what seemed to be a slender vine, dangling from one of the trees, change into a pale-green snake some eight feet long, whose strange head was prolonged into a slender, pointed beak. Even as the old man stared, it flashed across the deck not two feet away from him and disappeared in another tree. So perfectly did its color blend with the leaves that the instant it reached them it seemed to vanish from sight.

"It was the palm-snake," said Professor Ditson, after Jud told them of his experience. "It lives on lizards, and, although venomous, has never been known to bite a human being. If you had only been brave enough," he went on severely, "to catch it with your naked hand, we might even now have an invaluable record of the effects of its venom."

"What is the most venomous snake in the world?" broke in Will, as Jud tried to think of words strong enough to express what he thought of the scientist's suggestion.

"The hamadryad or king cobra," returned the professor. "I once secured one over fourteen feet long."

"How did you catch it?" queried Will.

"Well," said the professor, "I came across it by a fortunate accident. I was collecting butterflies in India at a time of the year when it is especially pugnacious, and this particular snake dashed out of a thicket at me. It came so unexpectedly that I had to run for my life. It seems ridiculous that I should have done so," he went on apologetically, "but the bite of the hamadryad is absolutely fatal. This one gained on me so rapidly that I was at last compelled to plunge into a near-by pond, since this variety of snake never willingly enters water."

"What happened then?" inquired Will, as the scientist came to a full stop.

"When I reached the opposite shore, a quarter of a mile away, and was about to land," returned the professor, "out of the rushes this same snake reared up some six feet. With the rare intelligence which makes the hamadryad such a favorite among collectors, it had circled the lake and was waiting for me."

"Snappy work!" said Jud, shivering. "I can't think of any pleasanter finish to a good swim than to find a nice fourteen-foot snake waitin' for me. What did you do then?"

"I floated around in deep water until my assistant came and secured the snake with a forked stick. It is now in the New York Zoölogical Gardens at the Bronx," concluded the professor.

Jud drew a deep breath. "That reminds me," he said at last, "of a time I once had with a pizen snake when I was a young man. I was hoein' corn up on a side hill in Cornwall when I was about sixteen year old," he continued. "All on a sudden I heard a rattlin' an' down the hill in one of the furrows came rollin' a monstrous hoop-snake.

You know," he explained, "a hoop-snake has an ivory stinger in its tail an' rolls along the ground like a hoop, an' when it strikes it straightens out an' shoots through the air just like a spear."

"I know nothing of the kind," broke in Professor Ditson.

"Well," said Jud, unmoved by the interruption, "when I saw this snake a-rollin' an' a-rattlin' down the hill towards me, I dived under the fence an' put for home, leavin' my hoe stickin' up straight in the furrow. As I slid under the fence," he went on, "I heard a thud, an' looked back just in time to see the old hoop-snake shoot through the air an' stick its stinger deep into the hoe-handle. It sure was a pizen snake, all right," he went on, wagging his head solemnly. "When I came back, an hour or so later, the snake was gone, but that hoe-handle had swelled up pretty nigh as big as my leg."

There was a roar of laughter from Will and Joe, while Jud gazed mournfully out over the water. Professor Ditson was vastly indignant.

"I feel compelled to state," he said emphatically, "that there is no such thing as a hoop-snake and that no snake-venom would have any effect on a hoe-handle."

"Have it your way," said Jud. "It ain't very polite of you to doubt my snake story after I swallowed yours without a word."

At Manaos they left the steamer, and Professor Ditson bought for the party a *montaria,* a big native boat without a rudder, made of plank and propelled by narrow, pointed paddles. Although Hen and Pinto and the Professor were used to this kind of craft, it did not appeal at all favorably to the Northerners, who were accustomed to the light bark-canoes and broad-bladed paddles of the Northern Indians. Joe was especially scornful.

"This boat worse than a dug out," he objected. "It heavy and clumsy and paddles no good either."

"You'll find it goes all right on these rivers," Professor Ditson reassured him. "We only have a few hundred miles more, anyway before we strike the Trail."

Under the skilful handling of Hen and
Pinto, the montaria, although it seemed un-
wieldly, turned out to be a much better craft
than it looked; and when the Northerners
became used to the narrow paddles, the expedition made great headway, the boys finding the wide boat far more comfortable for
a long trip than the smaller, swifter canoe.

After a day, a night, and another day of
paddling, they circled a wide bend, and there,
showing like ink in the moonlight, was the
mouth of another river.

"White men call it Rio Negros, Black
River," the Indian explained to the boys;
"but my people call it the River of Death."

As the professor, who was steering with a
paddle, swung the prow of the boat into the
dark water, the Indian protested earnestly.

"It very bad luck, Master to enter Death
River by night," he said.

"Murucututu, murucututu," muttered the
witch-owl, from an overhanging branch.

Hen joined in Pinto's protest.

"That owl be layin' a spell on us, Boss," he
said. "Better wait till mornin'."

The professor was inflexible.

"I have no patience with any such superstitions," he said. We can cover fully twenty-five miles before morning."

The Mundurucu shook his head and said nothing more, but Hen continued his protests, even while paddling.

"Never knew any good luck to come when that ol' owl's around," he remarked mournfully. "It was him that sicked them vampires on to Will here, an' we're all in for a black time on this black ribber."

"Henry," remarked Professor Ditson, acridly, "kindly close your mouth tightly and breathe through your nose for the next two hours. Your conversation is inconsequential."

"Yassah, yassah," responded Hen, meekly, and the montaria sped along through inky shadows and the silver reaches of the new river in silence.

About midnight the forest became so dense that it was impossible to follow the channel safely, and the professor ordered the boat to be anchored for the night. Usually it was possible to make a landing and camp on shore, but to-night in the thick blackness of the shadowed bank, it was impossible to see anything. Accordingly, the party, swathed in mosquito-netting, slept as best they could in the montaria itself.

It was at the gray hour before dawn, when men sleep soundest, that Jud was awakened by hearing a heavy thud against the side of the boat close to his head. It was repeated, and in the half-light the old man sat up. Once again came the heavy thud, and then, seemingly suspended in the air above the side of the boat close to his head, hung a head of horror. Slowly it thrust itself higher and higher, until, towering over the side of the boat, showed the fixed gleaming eyes and the darting forked tongue of a monstrous serpent. Paralyzed for a moment by his horror for all snake-kind, the old man could not move, and held his breath until the blood drummed in his ears. Only when the hideous head curved downward toward Joe did Jud recover control of himself. His prisoned voice came out then with a yell like a steam-siren, and he fumbled under his left armpit for the automatic revolver which he wore in the wilderness, night and day, strapped there in a waterproof case.

"Sucuruju! Sucuruju! Sucuruju!" shouted Pinto, aroused by Jud's yell. "The Spirit of the River is upon us!" And he grasped his machete just as Jud loosened his revolver.

Quick as they were, the huge anaconda, whose family includes the largest water-snakes of the world, was even quicker. With a quick dart of its head, it fixed its long curved teeth in the shoulder of the sleeping boy, and in an instant, some twenty feet of glistening coils glided over the side of the boat. The scales of the monster shone like burnished steel, and it was of enormous girth in the middle, tapering off at either end. Jud dared not shoot at the creature's head for fear of wounding Joe, but sent bullets as fast as he could pull the trigger into the great girth, which tipped the heavy boat over until the water nearly touched the gunwale. Pinto slashed with all his might with his machete at the back of the great snake, but it was like attempting to cut through steel-studded leather. In spite of the attack, the coils of the great serpent moved toward the boy, who, without a sound, struggled to release his shoulder from the terrible grip of the curved teeth. The anaconda, the sucuruju of the natives, rarely ever attacks a man; but when it does, it is with difficulty driven away. This one, in spite of steel and bullets, persisted in its attempt to engulf the body of the struggling boy in its coils, solid masses of muscle powerful enough to break every bone in Joe's body.

It was Hen Pine who finally saved the boy's life. Awakened by the sound of the shots and the shouts of Jud and Pinto, he reached Joe just as one of the fatal coils was half around him. With his bare hands he caught hold of both of the fierce jaws and with one tremendous wrench of his vast arms literally tore them apart. Released from their death grip, Joe rolled to one side, out of danger. The great snake hissed fiercely, and its deadly, lidless eyes glared into those of the man. Slowly, with straining, knotted muscles, Hen wrenched the grim jaws farther and farther apart. Then bracing his vast forearms, he bowed his back in one tremendous effort that, in spite of the steel-wire muscles of the great serpent, bent its deadly jaws backward and tore them down the sides, ripping the tough, shimmering skin like so much paper. Slowly, with a wrench and a shudder, the great water-boa acknowledged defeat, and its vast body pierced, slashed, and torn, reluctantly slid over the side of the boat.

As Hen released his grip of the torn jaws, the form of the giant serpent showed mirrored for an instant against the moonlit water and then disappeared in the inky depths below. Joe's thick flannel shirt had saved his arm from any serious injury, but Professor Ditson washed out the gashes made by the sharp curved teeth with permanganate of potash, for the teeth of the boas and pythons, although not venomous, may bring on blood-poisoning, like the teeth of any wild animal. Jud was far more shaken by the adventure than Joe, who was as impassive as ever.

"Snakes, snakes, snakes!" he complained. "They live in the springs and pop up beside the paths and drop on you out of trees. Now they 're beginnin' to creep out of the water to kill us off in our sleep. What a country!"

"It 's the abundance of reptile life which makes South America so interesting and attractive," returned Professor Ditson, severely.

It was Pinto who prevented the inevitable and heated discussion between the elders of the party.

"Down where I come from," he said, "lives a big water-snake many times larger than this one, called the Guardian of the River. He at least seventy-five feet long. We feed him goats every week. My grandfather and his grandfather's grandfather knew him. Once," went on Pinto, "I found him coiled up beside the river in such a big heap that I could n't see over the top of the coils."

"I don't know which is the worse," murmured Jud to Will, "seein' the snakes which *are* or hearin' about the snakes which *ain't*. Between the two, I'm gettin' all wore out."

Then Pinto went back again to his predictions about the river they were on.

"This river," he said, " is not called the

River of Death for nothing.   The old men of my tribe say that always dangers come here by threes.   One is passed, but two more are yet to come.   Never, Master, should we have entered this river by night."

"Yes," chimed in Hen, "when I heered that ol' witch-owl I says to myself, 'Hen Pine, there'll be somethin' bad a-doin' soon.'"

"You talk like a couple of superstitious old women," returned Professor Ditson, irritably.

"You wait," replied the Indian, stubbornly; "two more evils yet to come."

Pinto's prophecy was partly fulfilled with startling suddenness.   The party had finished breakfast, and the montaria was anchored in a smooth, muddy lagoon which led from the river back some distance into the forest. While Will and Hen fished from the bow of the boat the rest of the party curled themselves up under the shade of the overhanging trees to make up their lost sleep.   At first, the fish bit well and the two caught a number which looked much like the black bass of northern waters.   A minute later, a school of fresh-water flying-fish broke water near them and flashed through the air for a full twenty yards, like a flight of gleaming birds.

As the sun burned up the morning mist, it changed from a sullen red to a dazzling gold and at last to a molten white, and the two fishermen nodded over their poles as little waves of heat ran across the still water and seemed to weigh down their eyelids like swathings of soft wool. The prow of the boat swung lazily back and forth in the slow current which set in from the main river. Suddenly the dark water around the boat was muddied and discolored, as if something had stirred up the bottom ten feet below. Then up through the clouded water drifted a vast, spectral, grayish-white shape. Nearer and nearer to the suface it came, while Hen and Will dozed over their poles. Will sat directly in the bow, and his body, sagging with sleep, leaned slightly over the gunwale.

Suddenly the surface of the water was broken by a tremendous splash, and out from its depth shot half the body of a fish nearly ten feet in length. Its color was the gray-white of the ooze at the bottom of the

stream in which it had lain hidden until at-
tracted to the surface by the shadow of the
montaria drifting above him. Will awakened
at the hoarse shout from Hen just in time to
see yawning in front of him a mouth more
enormous than he believed any created thing
possessed outside of the whale family. It
was a full five feet between the yawning jaws,
which were circled by a set of small sharp
teeth. Even as he sprang back, the monster
lunged forward right across the edge of the
boat and the jaws snapped shut.

Will rolled to one side in an effort to escape
the menancing depths, and although he managed to save his head and body from the maw
of the great fish, yet the jaws closed firmly on
both his extended arms, engulfing them clear
to the shoulder. The little teeth, tiny in comparison with the size of the jaws in which they
were set, hardly more than penetrated the
sleeves of his flannel shirt and pricked the
skin below, but as the monster lurched backward toward the water its great weight drew
the boy irresistibly toward the edge of the
boat, although he dug his feet into the thwarts

and twined them around the seat on which he had been sitting. Once in the river, the fatal jaws would open again, and he felt that he would be swallowed as easily as a pike would take in a minnow.

Even as he was dragged forward to what seemed certain death, Will did not fail to recognize a familiar outline in the vast fish-face against which he was held. The small, deep-set eyes, the skin like oiled leather, long filaments extending from the side of the jaw, and the enormous round head were nothing more than that of the catfish or bullhead which he used to catch at night behind the mill-dam in Cornwall, enlarged a thousand times.

Although the monster, in spite of its unwieldy size, had sprung forth, gripped its intended prey, and started back for the water in a flash, yet Hen Pine was even quicker. In spite of his size, there was no one in the party quicker in an emergency than the giant negro. Even as he sprang to his feet he disengaged the huge steel machete which always dangled from his belt. Hen's blade, which he used as a bush-hook and a weapon, was half again as heavy as the ordinary machete, and he always kept it ground to a razor edge. He reached the bow just as the great, gray, glistening body slipped back over the gunwale, dragging Will irresistibly with it. Swinging the broad heavy blade over his head, with every ounce of effort in his brawny body, Hen, brought the keen edge down slantwise across the gray back of the river-monster, which tapered absurdly small in comparison with the vast spread of the gaping jaws. It was such a blow as Richard the Lion-hearted might have struck; and just as his historic battle-sword would shear through triple steel plate and flesh and bone, so that day the machete of Hen Pine, unsung in song or story, cut through the smooth gray skin, the solid flesh beneath, and whizzed straight on through the cartilaginous joints of the great fish's spine, nor ever stopped until it had sunk deep into the wood of the high gunwale of the boat itself. With a gasping sigh, the monster's head rolled off the edge of the boat and slowly sank through the dark water, leaving the long, severed trunk floating on the surface.

Reaching out, the negro caught the latter by one of the back fins and secured it with a quick twist of a near-by rope.

"That's the biggest piraiba I ever see," he announced. "They're fine to eat, an' turn about is fair play. Ol' piraiba try to eat you; now you eat him." And while Will sat back on the seat, sick and faint from his narrow escape, Hen proceeded to haul the black trunk aboard and carve steaks of the white, firm-set flesh from it.

"Every year along the Madeira River this fish tip over canoes and swallow Indians. They's more afraid of it," Hen said, "than they is of alligators or anacondas."

When Hen woke up the rest of the party and told them of the near-tragedy Pinto croaked like a raven.

"Sucuruju one, piraiba two; but three is yet to come," he finished despondingly. The next two days, however, seemed to indicate that the River had exhausted its malice against the travelers. The party paddled through a panorama of sights and sounds new to the Northerners, and at night camped safely on high, dry places on the banks.   On the morning of the third day the whole party started down the river before daylight and watched the dawn of a tropical day, a miracle even more beautiful than the sunrises of the North. One moment there was perfect blackness; then a faint light showed in the east; and suddenly, without the slow changes of Northern skies, the whole east turned a lovely azure blue, against which showed a film and fretwork of white clouds, like wisps of snowy lace.

Just as the sun came up they passed a tall and towering conical rock which shot up three hundred feet among the trees and terminated in what looked like a hollowed summit. Pinto told them that this was Treasure Rock, and that nearly half a thousand years ago the Spaniards, in the days when they were the cruel conquerors of the New World, had explored this river.   From the ancestors of Pinto's nation and from many another lesser Indian tribe they had carried off a great treasure of gold and emeralds and diamonds.

Not satisfied with these, they had tried to enslave the Indians and make them hunt for more. Finally, in desperation the tribes united, stormed their persecutors' camp, killed some, and forced the rest to flee down the river in canoes. When the Spaniards reached the rock, they landed, and, driving iron spikes at intervals up its steep side, managed to clamber up to the very crest and haul their treasure and stores of water and provisions after them by ropes made of lianas. There, safe from the arrows of their pursuers in the hollow top, they stood siege until the winter rains began. Then, despairing of taking the fortress, the Indians returned to their villages; whereupon the Spaniards clambered down, the last man breaking off the iron spikes as he came, and escaped to the Spanish settlements. Behind them, in the inaccessible bowl on the tip-top of the rock, they left their treasure-chest, expecting to return with the reinforcements and rescue it. The years went by and the Spaniards came not again to Black River, but generation after generation of Indians handed down the legend of Treasure Rock, with the iron-bound chest on its top, awaiting him who can scale its height.

Jud, a treasure-hunter by nature, was much impressed by Pinto's story.

"What do you think of takin' a week off and lookin' into this treasure business?" he suggested. "I'll undertake to get a rope over the top of this rock by a kite, or somethin' of that sort, an' then I know a young chap by the name of Adams who would climb up there an' bring down a trunk full of gold an' gems. What do you say?"

"Pooh!" is what Professor Amandus Ditson said, and the expedition proceeded in spite of Jud's protests.

CHAPTER V

SHIPWRECK

ABOUT the middle of the morning there sounded through the still air a distant boom, which grew louder until finally it became a crashing roar. Beyond a bend in the river stretched before them a long gorge. There the stream had narrowed, and, rushing across a ledge shaped like a horseshoe, foamed and roared and beat its way among the great boulders. The paddlers brought their craft into smooth water under an overhanging bank while they held a council of war. Professor Ditson had never been on the Rio Negros before, nor had Pinto followed it farther than Treasure Rock. For a long time the whole party carefully studied the distant rapids.

"What do you think?" whispered Will to Joe.

The Indian boy, who had paddled long journeys on the rivers and seas of the far Northwest, shook his head doubtfully.

"Can do in a bark canoe," he said at last; "but in this thing—I don't know."

Pinto and Hen both feared the worst in regard to anything which had to do with Black River. It was Professor Ditson who finally made the decision.

"'It would take us weeks," he said, "to cut a trail through the forests and portage this boat around. One must take some chances in life. There seems to be a channel through the very center of the horseshoe. Let's go!"

For the first time during the whole trip old Jud looked at his rival admiringly.

"The old bird has some pep left, after all," he whispered to Will. "I want to tell you, boy," he went on, "that I've never seen worse rapids, an' if we bring this canal-boat through, it'll be more good luck than good management."

Under Professor Ditson's instructions, Pinto took the bow paddle, while Hen paddled stern, with Will and Joe on one side and

Jud and the professor on the other. Then all the belongings of the party were shifted so as to ballast the unwieldy craft as well as possible, and in another moment they shot out into the swift current. Faster and faster the trees and banks flashed by, like the screen of a motion picture. Not even a fleck of foam broke the glassy surface of the swirling current. With smooth, increasing speed, the river raced toward the rapids which roared and foamed ahead, while swaying wreaths of white mist, shot through with rainbow colors, floated above the welter of raging waters and the roar of the river rose to shout. Beyond, a black horseshoe of rock stretched from one bank to the other in a half-circle, and in front of it sharp ridges and snags showed like black fangs slavered with the foam of the river's madness.

In another second the boat shot into the very grip of these jaws of death. Standing with his lithe, copper-colored body etched against the foam of the rapids, the Mundurucu held the lives of every one of the party in his slim, powerful hands. Accustomed from boyhood to the handling of the river-boats of his tribe through the most dangerous of waters, he stood that day like the leader of an orchestra, directing every movement of those behind him, with his paddle for a baton. Only a crew of the most skilled paddlers had a chance in that wild water; and such a crew was obedient to the Indian. In the stern, the vast strength of the giant negro swung the montaria into the course which the bow paddler indicated by his motions, while the other four, watching his every movement, were quick to paddle or to back on their respective sides. At times, as an unexpected rock jutted up before him in the foam, the Indian would plunge his paddle slantwise against the current and would hold the boat there for a second, until the paddlers could swing it, as on a fulcrum, out of danger. Once the craft was swept with tremendous force directly at an immense boulder, against which the water surged and broke.

To Jud and the boys it seemed as if Pinto had suddenly lost his control of the montaria, for, instead of trying to swing out of the grip of the currents that rushed upon the rock, he

steered directly at its face. The Mundurucu,
however, knew his business. Even as Jud
tensed his muscles for the crash, the rebound
and undertow of the waters, hurled back from
the face of the rock, caught the boat and
whirled it safely to one side of the boulder.
In and out among the reefs and fangs of rock
the Mundurucu threaded the boat so deftly,
and so well did his crew behind him respond,
that in all that tumult of dashing waves the
heavy craft shipped no water outside of the
flying spray.

In another minute they were clear of the
outlying reefs and ledges and speeding toward the single opening in the black jaw of
rock that lay ahead of them. Here it was
that, through no fault of their steersman, the
great mishap of the day overtook them. Just
beyond the gap in the rock was a little fall,
not five feet high, hidden by the spray. As
Pinto passed through the narrow opening he
swung the bow of the boat diagonally so as to
catch the smoother current toward the right-
hand bank of the river, which at this point
jutted far out into the rapids. As he

swerved, the long montaria shot through the air over the fall. The Indian tried to straighten his course, but it was too late. In an instant the boat had struck at an angle the rushing water beyond, with a force that nearly drove it below the surface. Before it could right itself, the rush of the current from behind struck it broadside, and in another second the montaria, half-filled with the water which it had shipped, capsized, and its crew were struggling in the current.

It was Hen Pine who reached the river first. When he saw that the boat was certain to upset he realized that his only chance for life was to reach smooth water. Even while the montaria was still in mid-air he sprang far out toward the bank, where a stretch of unbroken current set in toward a tiny cape, beyond which it doubled back into a chaos of tossing, foaming water where not even the strongest swimmer would have a chance for life. Hen swam with every atom of his tremendous strength, in order to reach that point before he was swept into the rapids beyond. His bare black arms and vast shoulders, knotted and ridged with muscle, thrashed through the water with the thrust of a propeller-blade as he swam the river-crawl which he had learned from Indian swimmers. For an instant it seemed as if he would lose, for when nearly abreast of the little cape several feet of racing current still lay between him and safety. Sinking his head far under the water, he put every ounce of strength into three strokes, the last of which shot him just near enough to the bank to grip a tough liana which dangled like a rope from an overhanging tree-top. Pinto, who was next, although no mean swimmer, would never have made the full distance, yet managed to grasp one of Hen's brawny legs, which stretched far out into the current.

"You hold on," he muttered to the great negro; "we make a monkey-bridge and save them all."

Hen only nodded his head and took a double turn of the lianas around each arm. Professor Ditson was the next one to win safety, for the two boys were staying by Jud, who was a most indifferent swimmer. As the professor's long, thin legs dangled out into the current like a pair of tongs, with a desperate stroke Will caught one of his ankles, and was gripped in turn by Joe, and Jud locked both of his arms around the latter's knees, while the swift river tossed his gray hair and beard along its surface. As the full force of the current caught this human chain it stretched and sagged ominously. Then each link tightened up and prepared to hold as long as flesh and blood could stand the strain.

"Go ahead, Jud!" gasped Will over his shoulder; "pull yourself along until you get to shore; then Joe will follow, and then I. Only hurry—the professor won't be able to hold on much longer, nor Hen to stand the strain."

"Don't hurry on my account," sounded the precise voice of Professor Ditson above the roar of the waters. "I can hold on as long as any one." And as he spoke Will felt his gaunt body stiffen until it seemed all steel and whipcord.

"Same here!" bellowed Hen, his magnificent body stretched out through the water as if on a rack. "Take your time and come along careful."

In another minute the old trapper had pulled his way hand over hand along the living bridge until he too had a grip on one of the dangling lianas. He was followed by link after link of the human chain until they were all safe at the edge of the bank. Hen was the first to scramble up and give the others a helping hand, and a moment later all six of the treasure-seekers stood safe on the high ridge of the little promontory and sadly watched the boat which had borne them so well smash into a mass of floating, battered planks among the rocks and disappear down the current. Along with it went their guns, their ammunition, and their supplies.

Jud alone retained the automatic revolver which he always wore, with a couple of clips holding sixteen cartridges, besides the eight in the cylinder. Hen also could not be termed weaponless, for he still wore his machete; while Will had a belt-ax, Joe a light hatchet, and Professor Ditson a sheath-knife. Besides these, the Indian had his bamboo tinder-box and flint and steel, which he always wore in his belt. These and the jack-knives and a few miscellaneous articles which they happened to have in their pockets or fastened to their belts comprised the whole equipment of the party.

Before them stretched a hundred miles of uncharted jungle, infested by dangerous beasts and wandering cannibal tribes, through which they must pass to reach the old Slave Trail. Half that distance behind them was the Amazon. If once they could find their way back to that great river and camp on its banks, sooner or later a boat would go by which would take them back to Manaos. This, however, might mean weeks of delay and perhaps the abandonment of the whole trip. As they stood upon a white sand-bank far enough back from the river so that the roar of the rapids no longer deafened them, it was Pinto who spoke first.

"Master," he said to Professor Ditson, "it is no time for council. Let us have fire and food first. A man thinks more wisely with his head when his stomach is warm and full."

"I 'll say the man is right," said Jud, shivering a little in his wet clothes as the coolness of the approaching night began to be felt through the forest; "but where is that same fire and food goin' to come from?"

Pinto's answer was to scrape shavings from the midrib of a dry palm-leaf. When he had a little pile on the white sand in front of him, he opened the same kind of tinder-box that our ancestors used to carry less than a century and a half ago. Taking out from this an old file and a bit of black flint, with a quick glancing blow he sent half a dozen sparks against a dry strip of feltlike substance found only in the nests of certain kinds of ants. In a minute a deep glow showed from the end of this tinder, and, placing it under the pile of shavings, Pinto blew until the whole heap was in a light blaze. Hastily piling dry wood on top of this, he left to the others the task of keeping the fire going and, followed by Will, hurried through the jungle toward the towering fronds of a peach-palm, which showed above the other trees. Twisting together two or three lianas, the Indian made from them a light, strong belt. This he slipped around himself and the tree, and, gripping it in both hands, began to walk up the rough trunk, leaning against this girdle and pushing it up with each step, until, sixty feet from the ground, he came to where the fruit of the tree was clustered at its top. It grew in a group of six, each one looking like a gigantic, rosy peach a foot in diameter. In a moment they all came whizzing to the ground, and the two staggered back to the fire with the party's supper on their backs. Stripping off the thick husk, Pinto exposed a soft kernel which, when roasted on the coals, tasted like a delicious mixture of cheese and chestnuts.

When at last all the members of the party were full-fed and dry, the wisdom of Pinto's counsel was evident. Every one was an optimist; and, after all, the best advice in life comes from optimists. Even Pinto and Hen felt that, now that they had lived through the third misfortune, they need expect no further ill luck from the river.

"Forward or back—which!" was the way Professor Ditson put the question.

"Forward!" voted Will.

"Forward!" grunted Joe.

Jud seemed less positive.

"I sure would hate to go back," he said, "after old Jim Donegan had grub-staked us, an' tell the old man that, while we 're good pearlers, we 're a total loss when it comes to emeralds. Yet," he went on judicially, "there 's a hundred miles of unexplored forests between us and the perfesser's trail, if there is any such thing. We 've lost our guns; we 've no provisions; we 're likely to run across bands of roving cannibals; lastly, it may take us months to cut our way through this jungle. Therefore I vote—forward!"

"That 's the stuff, Jud!" exclaimed Will, much relieved.

"Oh, I don't believe in takin' any chances," returned the old man, who had never done anything else all his life. "My idea is to always look at the dangers—an' then go ahead."

"What about me?" objected Hen. "I ain't a-goin' to cut no hundred miles of trail through this here jungle for nobody."

The answer came, sudden and unexpected, from the forests.

"John cut wood! John cut wood! John cut wood!" called some one, clearly. It was only a spotted goatsucker, a bird belonging to the same family as our northern whip-poor-will, but Hen was much amused.

"You hear what the bird say, you John Pinto. Get busy and cut wood," he laughed, slapping his friend mightily on the back.

"All right," said the Indian, smiling, "John *will* cut wood. Master," he said to Professor Ditson, "if all will help, I can make a montaria in less than a week, better than the one we lost. Then we not have to cut our way through jungle."

"Pinto," said Professor Ditson, solemnly, for once dropping into slang, "the sense of this meeting is—that you go to it."

That night they followed the bank until they found a place where it curved upward into a high, dry bluff. There, on soft white sand above the mosquito-belt, they slept the sleep of exhaustion. It was after midnight when Will, who was sleeping between Professor Ditson and Jud, suddenly awoke with a start. Something had sniffed at his face.

Without moving, he opened his eyes and looked directly into a pair that flamed green through the darkness. In the half-light of the setting moon he saw, standing almost over him, a heavily built animal as big as a small lion. Yet the short, upcurved tail and the rosettes of black against the gold of his skin showed the visitor to be none other than that terror of the jungle, the great jaguar, which in pioneer days used to come as far north as Arkansas and is infinitely more to be feared than the panthers which our forefathers dreaded so. This one had none of the lithe grace of the cougars which Will had met during the quest of the Blue Pearl, but gave him the same impression of stern tremendous strength and girth that a lion possesses.

All of these details came to Will the next day. At that moment, as he saw the great round head of this king of the South American forest within a foot of his own, he was probably the worst scared boy on the South American continent. Will knew that a jaguar was able to drag a full-grown ox over a mile, and that this one could seize him by the throat, flirt his body over one shoulder, and disappear in the jungle almost before he could cry out. The great beast seemed, however, to be only mildly interested in him. Probably he had fed earlier in the evening.

Even as Will stared aghast into the gleaming eyes of the great cat, he saw, out of the corner of his eye, Jud's right hand stealing toward his left shoulder. The old trapper, as usual, was wide awake when any danger threatened. Before, however, he had time to reach his automatic, Professor Ditson, equally watchful from his side, suddenly clapped his hands together sharply, close to the jaguar's pricked-up ears. The effect was instantaneous. With a growl of alarm, the great beast sprang backward and disappeared like a shadow into the forest.

The professor sat up.

"That's the way to handle jaguars," he remarked. "He'll not come back. If you had shot him," he continued severely to Jud, who held his cocked revolver in one hand, "he

would have killed the boy and both of us before he died himself." And the professor lay
down again to resume his interrupted slum-
bers.

It was this occurrence which started a discussion the next morning in regard to
weapons, offensive and defensive.

"I 'low," said Hen Pine, making his heavy
machete swing through the air as he whirled
it around his head, "that I can stop anything I
meet with this 'ere toothpick of mine."

"Hen," remarked Jud, impressively, "do
you see that round thing hangin' against the
sky in the big tree about fifty yards away?"

"Yassah, yassah," responded Hen, "that's a
monkey-pot full of Brazil-nuts."

"Well, boy," returned the old trapper,
"just keep your eye on it."

As he spoke he raised his automatic to the
level of his hip, shooting without sighting,
with that strange sixth sense of position which
some of the great revolver-shots of a past
generation used to acquire. There was a
flash, a sharp spat, and the case of nuts about
twice the size of a man's fist came whizzing to

the ground. Hen stared at the old trapper with his mouth open.

"You is sure the hittenest shooter ever I see," he said at last.

Joe said nothing, but, drawing from his belt the keen little hatchet which he always carried, poised himself with his left foot forward, and, whirling the little weapon over his head, sent it hurtling through the air toward the same Brazil-nut tree. The little ax buzzed like a bee and, describing a high curve, buried itself clear to the head in the soft bark. Picking up a couple of heavy round stones, Will put himself into a pitching position and sent one whizzing in a low straight peg which hardly rose at all and which struck the tree close to Joe's hatchet with a smack which would have meant a broken bone for any man or beast that it struck; for, as Joe had found out when the two were pursued by Scar Dawson's gang, Will was a natural-born stone-thrower, with deadly speed and accuracy.

It was Professor Ditson, however, who gave what was perhaps the most spectacular exhibition of all. Standing before them, lean and gaunt, he suddenly reached to his belt and drew out a keen, bone-handled, double-edged sheath-knife. Poising this flat on the palm of his hand, he threw it, with a quick jerk, with much the same motion of a cricket-bowler. The keen weapon hissed through the air like an arrow, and was found sunk nearly to the hilt in the bark between the mark of Will's stone and the head of Joe's hatchet.

"When I was a very young man," the professor explained, embarrassed, "I attained a certain amount of proficiency with the bowie-knife."

"I 'll say you did!" exclaimed Jud, as he worked the knife out of the tough bark. "Any cannibal that comes within fifty yards of this party is liable to be chopped an' stabbed an' broken an' shot—to say nothin' of Hen's machete at close quarters."

Pinto had watched these various performances in silence.

"This evening," he said at last, "I show you a gun that kills without any noise."

Borrowing Joe's hatchet, he disappeared into the woods, to come back half an hour later with a nine-foot stick of some hard, hollow, light wood about an inch in diameter, straight as an arrow, and with a center of soft pith. Laying this down on a hard stump, Pinto, with the utmost care, split the whole length into halves. Then, fumbling in his belt he pulled from it one of the sharp teeth of the paca, that curious reddish rodent which is half-way in size and appearance between a hog and a hare and which is equally at home on land and in water, and whose two-inch cutting-teeth are among the favorite ready-made tools of all South American Indians. With one of these Pinto carefully hollowed out each section of the stick, smoothing and polishing the concave surface until it was like glass. Then, fitting the two halves together, he wound them spirally with a long strip of tape which he made from the tough, supple wood of a climbing palm, waxed with the black wax of the stingless bees. When it was finished he had a light, hollow tube about nine feet long. At one end, which he tapered slightly, he fixed, upright, the tiny tooth of a mouse, which he pressed down until only a fleck of shining ivory showed as a sight above the black surface of the tube. At the other end he fitted in a cup-shaped mouthpiece, chiseled out of a bit of light, seasoned wood.

By noon it was finished, and Jud and the boys saw for the first time the deadly blow-gun of the Mundurucu Indians. For arrows, Pinto cut tiny strips from the flinty leaf-stalks of palm-leaves. These he scraped until the end of each was as sharp as a needle. Then he feathered them with little oval masses of silk from the seed-vessels of silk-cotton trees, whose silk is much fluffier and only about half the weight of ordinary cotton. In a short time he had made a couple of dozen of these arrows, each one of which fitted exactly to the bore of the blow-gun, and also fashioned for himself a quiver of plaited grasses, which he wore suspended from his shoulder with a strip of the palm tape.

Late in the afternoon he made another trip into the forest, returning with a mass of bark scraped from a tree called by the Indians *ma-vacure,* but which the white settlers in South America have named the poison tree. This bark he wet in the river, and then pounded it between two stones into a mass of yellowish fibers, which he placed in a funnel made of a plantain-leaf. Under this he set one of the aluminum cups which each of the party carried fastened to his belt. This done, he poured in cold water and let the mass drip until the cup was full of a yellow liquid, which he heated over a slow fire. When it thickened he poured in some of the milky juice of another near-by tree, which turned the mixture black. When it had boiled down to a thick gummy mass, Pinto wrapped it up carefully in a palm-leaf, after first dipping every one of his arrows into the black compound.

So ended the making of the famous urari arrow-poison, which few white men indeed have ever seen brewed. When it was safely put away, Pinto carefully fitted one of the tiny arrows into the mouthpiece and raised the blow-gun to his mouth, holding it with both hands touching each other just beyond the mouthpiece, instead of extending his left arm, as a white man would hold a gun. Even as he raised the long tube, there came a crashing through the near-by trees, and the party looked up to see a strange sight. Rushing along the branches came a pale greenish-gray lizard, marked on the sides with black bars and fully six feet in length. Along its back ran a crest of erect spines. Even as its long compressed tail whisked through the foilage, a reddish animal, which resembled a lanky raccoon, sprang after it like a squirrel, following hard on its trail.

"It's an' ol' coati chasin' a big iguana," muttered Hen, as the pair went by. "They're both mighty fine eatin'."

At first, the pursued and the pursuer seemed equally matched in speed. Little by little, the rapid bounds of the mammal overtook the swift glides of the reptile, and in a tree-top some fifty yards away the iguana turned at bay. In spite of its size and the threatening, horrible appearance of its uplifted spines, the coati made short work of it, worrying it like a dog, and finally breaking its spine. Even as its long bulk hung lifeless from the power-ful jaws of the animal, Pinto drew a deep breath and, sighting his long tube steadily to-

ward the distant animal, drove his breath
through the mouth-piece with all his force.
There followed a startling pop, and a white
speck flashed through the air toward the coati.
A second later, the latter, still holding the dead
iguana, gave a spring as if struck by something, and started off again through the tree-
tops, the great body of the dead lizard trailing behind. Suddenly the coati began to go
slower and slower and then stopped short. Its
head drooped. First one paw and then another relaxed, until, with a thud, the coati and
iguana struck the ground together both stone-
dead. The boys rushed over and found
Pinto's tiny, deadly arrow embedded deep in
the coati's side. Less than a minute had passed
since it had been struck, but the deadly urari
had done its work. Fortunately, this poison
does not impair the food value of game, and
later on, over a bed of coals, Hen made good
his words about their eating qualities. The
coati tasted like roast 'possum, while the flesh
of the giant lizard was as white and tender as
chicken.

"I feel as if I was eatin' a dragon," grumbled Jud, coming back for a third helping.

Followed a week of hard work for all.
Under Pinto's directions, taking turns with
Jud's ax, they cut down a yellow stone-
wood tree, which was almost as hard and
heavy as its name. Out of the trunk they
shaped a log some nineteen feet in length and
three feet through, which, with infinite pains
and with lianas for ropes, they dragged on
rollers to the water's edge. Then, with enormous labor, working by shifts with Joe's
hatchet, Jud's ax, and Hen's machete, they
managed to hollow out the great log. At
the end of the fourth day, Jud struck.

"I'll work as hard as any man," he said,
"but I got to have meat. If I work much
longer on palm-nuts I'm liable to go plumb
nutty myself."

As the rest of the party felt the same crav-
ing, Pinto and Jud were told off to hunt for
the rest of that day. It was Jud who first
came across game, a scant half-mile from
camp, meeting there an animal which is one
of the strangest still left on earth and which,
along with the duck-bill of Australia and the

great armadillo, really belongs to a past age, before man came to earth, but by some strange accident has survived to this day.

In front of him, digging in a dry bank with enormous curved claws, was an animal over six feet in length and about two feet in height. It had great hairy legs, and a tremendous bushy tail, like a vast plume, curled over its back. Its head ended in a long, tapering, toothless snout, from which was thrust constantly a wormlike, flickering tongue, while a broad oblique stripe, half gray and half black, showed on either side.

"There ain't no such animal," murmured Jud to himself, examining the stranger with awe.

Pinto's face shone with pleasure when he came up.

"It giant ant-eater and very good to eat," he remarked cheerfully.

Upon seeing them, the great beast shuffled away, but was soon brought to bay, when it stood with its back against the bank, swinging its long snout back and forth and making a little whining noise. Jud was about to step in and kill it with a blow from his ax, but Pinto held him back.

"No get in close to ant-bear," he warned, pointing to the giant's claws. "He rip you to pieces. You watch."

Stepping back, the Indian raised his blow-gun to his mouth. Again came the fatal pop, and the next second one of the tiny arrows was embedded like a thorn in the side of the monster's snout. For a moment the great ant-eater tried to dislodge the tiny pointed shaft with his enormous claws. Then he stopped, stood motionless for a while, swayed from side to side, and sank dead without a sound or struggle. With the help of Jud's ax and his own knife, the Indian soon quartered and dressed the great beast and an hour later the two staggered back to camp loaded down with a supply of meat which, when roasted, tasted much like tender pork.

"Now," said Jud, smacking his lips after a full meal, "bring on your work!"

CHAPTER VI

THE BLACK TIGER

UNDER Pinto's direction the hollow trunk was lifted up so that each end rested on a stump. Then a slow fire was kindled under its whole length. Pinto tended this most carefully, so that the heat would spread evenly. Gradually, under the blaze, the green wood spread out. This was the most critical point in this forest boat-building, for if there were too much heat at any one point, a crack might start through the log and all the work of the week go for nothing. As the great log opened out, the Indian moved constantly up and down its length, checking the blaze here and there with wet moss where the sides were spreading out too fast. At several different points he fitted in straddlers, with wedges made from stone-wood branches. By skilfully changing the pressure of these and varying the heat at different points the hollowed log at last took on a graceful curve, with tapered turned-up ends. Green strips of stonewood were fitted in for gunwales, and seats and semicircular end-boards put in place. Then the long dugout was allowed to cool off gradually all through one night. As it contracted, it locked in place gunwales, seats and thwarts. Another day was given to fashioning light paddles out of palm-wood; and then at last, one week after their shipwreck, these latter-day Argonauts were once more afloat upon Black River.

There followed long days, in each of which three seasons were perfectly reproduced. The mornings had all the chill of early spring; by noon came the blinding heat of midsummer; and the nights, of the same length as the days, had the frosty tang of autumn. During the morning of each day they paddled, lying by at noon-time in cool, shaded lagoons where they slept or fished. At other times they would collect nuts and fruits on the shore, under the direction of Professor Ditson, or take turns in going with

Pinto on short hunting-trips, during which all kinds of strange game would fall before his deadly blow-gun.

It was Jud who went with him on the first of these hunts. As they came to the bank of one of the many streams that ran into the Black River, the old trapper caught sight of a strange animal on the bank which looked like a great guinea-pig about the size of a sheep. Its wet hide was all shining black in the sunlight, and even as Jud turned to ask the Indian what it was, there sounded just behind him the fatal pop of the blow-gun, a venomous little arrow buzzed through the air, and a second later was sticking deep in the beast's blunt muzzle. Like an enormous muskrat, the stranger scrambled to the edge of the stream, plunged in, and disappeared in the dark water.

"That was a capybara," Pinto informed Jud.

"Well, you 've lost him all right, whatever he was," returned the latter.

"Wait," was all that Pinto would say.

A few minutes later, the limp, dead body

of the capybara, the largest of all aquatic rodents floated to the surface. Jud was about to wade into the shallow water and secure it when he was stopped by the Mundurucu.

"Never put your hand or foot into strange water," he said. "You may lose 'em."

Without explaining himself, he cut a long pole and carefully towed the dead animal to shore. That night the whole party camped on a high, dry, sandy bluff where Pinto and Hen dressed the capybara and roasted parts of it on long green spits of ironwood.

Will sampled the dank, dark meat cautiously.

"Tastes like a woodchuck I once tried to eat," he remarked, after one mouthful. "You can have my share." And he went back to palm-nuts.

From another trip, Pinto brought back a coaita, one of the spider-monkeys which had so affected Will's appetite on the occasion of their first meal at Professor Ditson's house. This one had a long, lank body covered with coarse black hair, while its spectral little face was set in a mass of white whiskers.

Will ate the rich, sweet meat shudderingly. "It looks just like a little old man," he protested.

"But it tastes better," observed the hardened Jud, passing his bark plate for another helping.

It was Jud and Will who accompanied Pinto on the third and most eventful trip of all. The boat had been beached at the slope of a high bank; and, while the others dozed or slept, Pinto and his two companions started through the woods on their hunt for any game which might add some kind of meat to their menu. A hundred yards from the bank the jungle deepened and darkened. Everywhere the strangler-fig was killing straight, slim palms and towering silk-cotton and paradise-nut trees. At first, this assassin among the tree-folk runs up its victim's trunk like a vine. As the years go by, it sends out shoots and stems around and around the tree it has chosen. These join and grow together, forming a vast hollow trunk, in the grip of which the other tree dies. Pools of black water showed here and there at the foot of the strangled trees, and something sinister seemed to hang over this stretch of jungle.

"Feels kind of creepy here," Jud confided to Will. "Looks just the kind of a place for some of Hen's haunts," he went on.

Even as he spoke, there sounded among the distant trees ominous grunting groans, and here and there among the shadows dark shapes could be seen moving about. The fierce moaning grew louder, mingled with a clicking noise like castanets.

"Peccaries!" muttered Jud. "I've hunted the little ones down in Mexico. They were liable to bite a piece out of you as big as a tea-cup. I'm in favor of lettin' these big fellows strictly alone."

"Quiet, quiet!" muttered the Indian, slipping behind a tree and motioning his companions to do likewise. "They go by in a minute, and I take off the last one with my blow-gun."

Instead of doing this, however, the great herd spread out through the woods, grunting and groaning and clattering their sharp tusks. As they came closer and closer, each of the peccaries seemed nearly as large as the wild boar of European forests, while their lips and lower jaws were pure white. The Mundurucu showed signs of alarm.

"Something has stirred them up," he muttered. "If they see us, they charge. Better each one choose a tree."

Even as he spoke, the leading peccary, whose gleaming tusks thrust out like keen knives from each side of his white jowl, glimpsed the little party in the shadows. With a deep groan, he lowered his head and charged at full speed, his tusks clattering as he came, while the white foam showed like snow against the raised bristles of his back. The whole herd followed—a nightmare of fierce heads, gleaming red eyes, and clicking, dagger-like tusks. Against such a rush Jud's automatic was as useless as Pinto's blow-gun or Will's throwing-stones. There was only one thing to do, and, with the utmost promptness all three of the party did it. Jud went up the vinelike trunk of a small strangler-fig hand over hand, nor ever stopped until he was safe astride the branch of a stonewood tree, twenty feet from the ground. Pinto, gripping the rough red bark of a cow tree, walked up it Indian fashion until he was safely seated in a crotch far above the ground. Will was not so fortunate. Near him was the smooth bark of an assai-palm. Twice he tried to climb it, and twice slipped back. Then, with every muscle tense, he dodged behind it and sprinted, as he had never run before, across a little opening to where a vast strangler-fig had swallowed a Brazil-nut tree in its octopus grip. The rush of the charging herd was hard on his heels as he reached the tree, and he had just time to swerve around its trunk and grip one of the vinelike tentacles which had not yet become a part of the solid shell of the strangler. Even as he swung himself from the ground, the bristling head of one of the herd struck against his feet, and he kicked them aloft just in time to avoid the quick double slash of the sharp tusks that followed.

Up and up he went, while the whole shell-like structure of the fig swayed and bent under his weight and dry dust from the dead nut tree powdered down upon him in showers.

Finally he reached a safe stopping-place, where he could stand with both feet resting in a loop which the snakelike fig had made in one of its twisting turns around its victim.

For a few minutes the trio in the tree-tops sat and stared in silence at one another and the weaving, champing herd of furious beasts below. It was Jud who spoke first.

"It's your move, Captain Pinto," he remarked. "What do we do next?"

"Sit still until they go away," returned the Indian despondently.

"How many arrows have you left?" inquired Will from his tree.

"Ten."

"I've got sixteen shots in my locker," observed Jud, from his perch; "but there must be nearly a hundred pigs in this herd; an' if these big fellows are like the chaps I knew in Mexico, the more you kill, the more those that are left will try to kill you."

"The only thing to do is to sit still," repeated the Mundurucu. "Perhaps they go 'way before night."

"Perhaps they don't, too," grumbled Jud.

"A pig's an obstinate critter at his best, an' a peccary's a pig at his worst!"

As time went on, conversation among the besieged flagged and each one settled down to endure the wait as best he might. Will amused himself by watching the birds which passed him among the tree-tops and listening to some of their strange and beautiful songs. At any time of the year and in any part of the world, a bird-student can always find pleasure in his hobby where unseeing, unhearing people find nothing of interest. To-day the first bird that caught his eye looked something like a crow, save that it had a crest of curved, hairy feathers, which at times, on its perch in a neighboring tree, it would raise and spread out over its head like a fringed parasol. From its breast swung a pad of feather-covered flesh, and, as it perched, it would every now and then give a deep low flute-note, raising its parasol each time in a most comical manner.

"What's that bird, Pinto?" Will inquired, after he had watched it delightedly for a long time.

"He umbrella-bird," returned the other, indifferently; "no good to eat." For the Mundurucu had a very simple system of ornithology—he divided all birds into two groups, those that were good to eat and those that were not.

The next bird which passed by aroused the interest even of Jud, who cared even less for birds than did the Indian. Through the dim light of the sinister forest, above the raging, swinish herd, flitted a bird of almost unearthly beauty, a parrot over three feet in length, of a soft, hyacinthine blue except around the eyes, where the bare skin showed white. As Will watched it delightedly, he recognized the bird as the hyacinthine macaw, the largest, most beautiful, and one of the rarest of all the parrot family. Even as he looked, the great bird alighted on a neighboring Brazil-nut tree and immediately showed itself to be as efficient as it was beautiful. Seizing in its great black beak one of the tough, thick nut-cases, called "monkey-pots" by the Indians, it proceeded to twist off its top and open up a side, although a man finds difficulty in doing this even with a hammer and chisel. Drawing out one Brazil-nut after another, it crushed them, in spite of their hard, thick shells, into a pulp, which it swallowed. Then it flew away, leaving Will staring regretfully after it.

As noon approached, the vines and the tree-trunks seemed to hold and radiate the heat like boiler-tubes. Gradually it rose and concentrated until the forest seemed to throb and pulsate like a furnace. Then a cicada began to sound. It began with a low, jarring note, something like the creaking of our ordinary katydid. This increased slowly in loudness and volume until at last it ended with an almost unendurable siren-whistle note which seemed to shake the very leaves of the trees. Again and again and again this performance was repeated, until Will, deafened and stunned by the noise, dizzy with the heat, and cramped and tired of standing on his narrow perch, thought with an almost unutterable longing of the dark, cool river and the shaded boat where the rest of the party were even now taking their noontide nap.

Suddenly, when it seemed to Will as if his

tortured brain absolutely could not stand one more repetition of this song, the talented cicada, with one farewell screech that surpassed all previous efforts, lay off for the day. For a few minutes there was almost complete silence in the darkened forest. Many of the guardian herd had laid down, wallowing in the soft mold and fallen leaves, while others, although they stared redly up into the treetops, no longer moved around and around in a circle of which the trapped hunters were the center. Suddenly, from the depths of a nearby tree, a pure, sweet, contralto voice sounded, as if some boy were singing to himself. For a moment it rose and fell, and then followed a few plaintive notes almost like those of a tiny flute. Then a slow melody began, full of mellow notes, only to be broken off abruptly. After a pause, there came a few clicking notes like those made by a music-box as it runs down, and the performance was over. Although the song came from the dark, glossy leaves of the very next tree, stare as he would, Will could gain no sight of the singer. Twice more the same thing happened. Each time he listened with a feeling that this time the tune would be finished and would be such as no mortal ears had heard before; but each time the song would die away in futile clicking notes. When at last the silence was again unbroken, Will turned toward the Indian.

"What was it, Pinto?" he asked softly.

"That organ-bird."

"What does it look like?"

"Don't know. No one ever see it."

"How do you know it's a bird?"

"Professor Ditson say so," returned Pinto, conclusively.

"That settles it," broke in Jud, jealously, from his tree. "He never saw it; nobody ever saw it; but the professor calls it an organ-bird. If he said it was an angel, I suppose it *would* be an angel."

"Yes," returned the Indian placidly.

The argument was suddenly ended for Will in a terrible manner. A sharp, burning pain shot through his left shoulder, as if a red-hot coal had been pressed there. As he turned, he saw, trickling down the tree-trunk, long crimson streams, one of which had already reached him, and he recognized, to his horror, a troop of the dreaded fire-ants. Even as he looked, the bites of several others pierced his skin, and the pain ran like a liquid poison through his veins as each blood-red ant rushed forward and buried its envenomed jaws deep into his flesh. Brushing off with frantic haste those torturers that had succeeded in reaching him, the boy began to slip down the vine toward the ground, for it was no more possible to resist this red torrent of poison and agony than it would be to stand against a creeping fire or a stream of molten lava.

Old Jud heard the involuntary cry, which the sudden pain had wrung from Will, and looked over, only to see the red columns of ants streaming slowly, inevitably down the tree, driving Will before them to what seemed certain death. The peccary herd, aroused by his movements, had gathered around the tree in close-packed ranks, and frothing, clattering, and moaning, waited for him, making a circle of gleaming tusks.

"Go back!" called out Jud. "Go back! You can't possibly get through 'em."

"I can't!" called back Will. "I 'd rather die fighting than be tortured to death up here."

As he spoke he slid another yard toward the ground. Jud drew in his breath in a gasp that was almost a groan, and, unslinging his ready automatic, began to scramble down to the ground."

"What you do?" called out the Indian, aghast, from his tree.

"I 'm a-goin' to stand by that kid," said the old trapper, grimly. "I 'll never go back to the boat alive without him."

"Stay where you are, Jud," shouted Will, desperately, as he gripped the keen hatchet which he had borrowed from Joe when he started on this ill-omened hunt.

"Come on, boy!" shouted the trapper, un-heedingly, as he neared the ground. "I 'll meet you, an' you fight through them to my tree. The old man 's a-goin' to be right with you."

His words were punctuated by the deadly pop of Pinto's blow-gun. Although the In-dian could not attain to Jud's height of self-sacrifice, yet he had made up his mind to do all that he could do to save the boy with the weapon he had. Again and again and again, as fast as he could level, load, and discharge his long blow-pipe, the fatal little arrows sped through the gloom and buried themselves in the thick hides of the peccaries. Already some of the inner ring were wavering and staggering under the effects of the deadly urari poison. The sight of their stricken comrades, however, only seemed to drive the herd into deeper depths of dumb, unreasoning madness. They pressed closer and closer to the tree, trampling their dead and dying comrades unheedingly underfoot, and the chorus of moaning grunts and clicking tusks sounded loud and louder.

The blood-red stream of fire-ants was half-way down the tree by this time, and Will was within a scant ten feet of the ground. The ants were very close as he lowered himself another yard, then a foot lower, and a foot beyond that, until the tusks of the plunging, leaping peccaries beneath him nearly touched his shoes. Bracing his feet against the rough trunk, he drew the little ax from his belt, and prepared to spring as far out toward Jud's tree as possible, although his heart sank and the flesh of his legs and thighs seemed to curl and chill as he looked out upon the gleaming ring of sharp, slashing tusks among which he must leap. Once downed by the herd, and he would be ripped to pieces before he could regain his feet.

Jud by this time was on the ground, and was just about to shoot, in an attempt to open a passage through the packed herd, when unexpected help came from above.

Out of the dark depths of a near-by silk-cotton tree sprang with silent swiftness a great black figure which gleamed in the half-light like watered silk.

"Look out! Look out! The black tiger!" shouted Pinto, despairingly, from his tree, having shot his last arrow into the frothing circle. Even as he spoke, the "tiger," as the Indians call the jaguar, landed full on the back and shoulders of the hindmost of the desperate, raging circle. As he landed, the great cat struck one blow with that terrible full stroke of a jaguar, which has been known to break the neck of an ox, and the peccary, with a shrill squeal of terror, went down before the death which haunts every peccary herd. At the squeal, the wild swine swung away from the tree with an instantaneous rush. A jaguar is to a peccary herd what the gray wolf is to the musk-ox of the north and the very life of each member of the herd depends upon facing their foe. Upon the instant, every peccary left the trees and hurried toward their dying comrade.

Unfortunately for the jaguar, the force of his spring, added to the impetus of his stroke, carried him too far, and for a moment he whirled over in a half-somersault and was entangled among the vines. Those lost seconds were fatal, in spite of all his strength and swiftness. Even as he recovered his feet in a lithe whirl and flirted over one shoulder the body of the dead peccary as a man might toss a rabbit, the death-ring formed around him. Two deep, the maddened swine circled him. With a deep, coughing roar, the tiger dropped his prey and struck with his armed paws light-ning-like blows that ripped the life out wherever they landed.   By this time, however, the peccaries were beyond all fear of death, and a score of them dashed in upon him. Jud had involuntarily leveled his automatic at the great brute as it struck the ground, but lowered it with a grim laugh.

"He's fightin' for our lives as well as his own," he called quietly to Will, as the latter reached the ground and slipped unnoticed past the heaving, tossing, fighting circle of peccaries. In another minute the boy had gained the safety of Jud's tree and gripped the old man's hand between his own.

"Let's stay here," said the old trapper, "an' see it out.   We can climb this tree if they come back, an' you'll never see a fight like this again."

Even as he spoke, the circle bent in upon the great cat. With desperate leaps, he tried to spring over its circumference; but each time it widened out so that always in front and at his back and on both flanks was a fence of sharp, slashing tusks. All around him lay dead peccaries which had fallen before his incredibly rapid strokes; but now his dark, gleaming skin was furrowed and slit with long bloody slashes where the tusks of dead and dying boars had gone home.   His strength ebbed with his blood.   Once more, with a deep, despairing roar, he struck with both paws, killing a peccary at each blow.   Then he staggered forward, and in a minute was down!

Time and again his great jaws opened and closed, sinking fierce white fangs deep through the skull or spine of some peccary, but at last only a black heaving of the furious wild pigs could be seen.   At times the dark, desperate head of the dying tiger thrust its way out, only to fall back, smothered and slashed.   Amid a scene of brute rage and fury which even Jud, old hunter as he was, had never imagined before, the little party slipped shudderingly away and hastened back over the trail along which they had come, nor ever stopped until they had reached the refuge of the montaria.   There they found the rest of the party peacefully sleeping through the midday hours under a cool canopy of broad green palm-leaves which Hen had thrown together. Professor Ditson was more interested in their description of the black tiger than in any of the other details of their adventure.

"It was the melanic type of the jaguar and very rare," he said regretfully. "It was certainly unfortunate that you could n't have collected this one, for there is no specimen, living or dead, in any of the zoölogical gardens or natural-history museums of the world."

"You see, Professor," explained Jud, "we were kind o' busy in keepin' some seventy-five peccaries from collectin' us. What does 'melanic' mean in American?"

"Any animal may develop either a black or a white type," explained the professor. "When black, it is called 'melanic'; when white, 'albino.' You probably have seen black squirrels, muskrats, or skunks. They are simply color-variations of the ordinary species. So this 'black tiger' was only a jaguar which for some unknown reason happened to have a black skin. These black examples," he continued, "are neither fiercer nor larger than the ordinary kind, although generally considered so by unscientific observers."

"What about some of those peccaries?" remarked Joe, practically. "Can't we bring in one or two that Pinto killed for fresh meat?"

"No, sir," returned Jud, emphatically, "I would n't go back into that black bit of woods for all the fresh peccary pork in South America."

It was Hen Pine who noted that Will had taken no part in the discussion, and that he was flushed and feverish and suffering intensely from the intolerable pain of the fire-ant bites.

"Honey, you come along with ol' Hen," he said soothingly, "an' he 'll fix you up so that you won't feel that fire-poison hurtin' any more."

Followed by Will, he led the way along the river-bank until they came to a small, round-topped tree with intensely green leaves. With his machete, Hen cut off several of the smaller branches. From the severed ends a thick, brilliant red sap oozed.

"It 's the dragon's-blood tree," he explained

"an' its juice makes the best balm in the world for burns or stings."

As he spoke he rubbed the thick, gummy liquid gently on the swollen and inflamed welts which the venomous bites of the fire-ants had raised on Will's shoulders and back. Almost instantly the throbbing, rankling pain stopped, and there came such a feeling of grateful coolness that Will told Hen it was almost worth the pain of the bite to feel the relief of the cure.

On the way back, Hen discovered another tree which brought the rest of the party nearly as much pleasure as the dragon's-blood had given to Will. It had long, glossy leaves, and a straight smooth trunk as large around as a man's body, though it was only about twenty feet high. It was loaded down with what looked like huge plums nearly the size of muskmelons. Hen told Will that it was the wild papaw tree. The fruit was delicious. When they brought back samples to the rest of the party, there was a stampede to the place and the boat was soon loaded with the luscious fruit.

As they explored the bank farther, Jud noticed that Hen was constantly chewing the dark green leaves of the wild cinnamon, which grew abundantly and had a spicy, pleasant smell like the well-known bark of that name. Without saying anything to Hen, the old man picked several and sampled them. Unfortunately for him, it takes prolonged practice to be able to chew wild cinnamon with any degree of comfort. As the fragrant fiery juice touched Jud's tongue and gums he gasped, the tears ran from his eyes as if he had swallowed red pepper, and he spat out the burning leaves emphatically.

"You must have a leather-lined mouth," he remarked to the grinning negro.

A little later, Hen added insult to the injury of the old trapper. They had come to a small tree loaded down with little round, rosy, fruit.

"That what you need, Mars' Jud," Hen assured him.

Thinking that it was perhaps a smaller edition of the papaw tree, Jud trustingly sank his teeth into one of the little spheres, only to find it bitter as gall.

"What do you mean by tellin' ·me I need anything that tastes like that," he howled.

"I did n't say for you to *eat* it," laughed the black giant. "I say you needed it. That tree the soap-tree," and Hen pointed to Jud's grimy hands suggestively.

"I guess we all need it," interrupted Will, tactfully, before Jud could express his indignation further.

Picking handfuls of the little fruit, each one of the party dipped his hands into a pool near the river bank. The waxy surface of the rosy balls dissolved in a froth of lather which left their hands as clean and white as the best of soap could have done.

As the day waned and the coolness of the late afternoon stole through the heat, the montaria was again loosed from the bank. All that night, under the light of another glorious full moon, they traveled fast and far. At last, just as the sun rose, there sounded a distant boom. It became louder and louder until the air quivered and the dark surface of the river showed here and there flecks and blobs of foam. Then, as they swept around a bend in the black stream, there appeared before them a sight of unearthly beauty not seen of white men for twice two hundred years.

CHAPTER VII

THE YELLOW SNAKE

OVER a vast horseshoe of towering crags, with a drumming roar, the dark, resistless river rushed in a mass of snowy foam and broken rainbows down into the whirling caldron below.

"The Falls of Utiarity," whispered Pinto, as he guided the boat into a little bend by the bank just above where the terrible downward glide of the river began. Making fast to a tree on shore, the whole party stared across at the most beautiful waterfall on earth, as if they could never see enough of its beauty. Something seemed to give way in Will's brain, and for a long minute he felt as if he were entering a new and strange world. Dim, unearthly images seemed to float before him. He thought of the great white throne in Revelation—the mystic emerald circled by a rainbow and the pavement of a single sapphire-stone. Before him was the beautiful water, sinking into the abyss, yet flowing on forever, while a great rainbow trembled, faded, then came again through the mist and spray like a beautiful spirit walking the waters. With the terror, the rush, and the roar of the crashing waters, was a beauty not of earth that took away all fear, until he seemed to be gazing into the seventh heaven and seeing that which was unlawful for mortal man to look upon.

Only a moment, and once more he was back in the body and found himself looking confusedly into the faces of his companions, all of whom had felt something of the same uplift. Without a word, the Indian edged the canoe along the shore and into the mouth of a deep lagoon, half-hidden by overhanging trees. Beyond these it widened out and ended in a high, bare bank. Back from this stretched a narrow path, showing like a long line through the dark green of the jungle. Its surface was trodden ominously hard and smooth, as if crossed and recrossed by many bare feet.

"The Trail," said Pinto, softly.

"The Trail," echoed Professor Ditson, as they all stared along the thin line which pierced the forest and led away and across the vast basin of the Amazon and on and past the guarded heights of Peru until it reached the mines from which Spain had dug the gold which enabled her to conquer and hold half the world. Only the cruel, fierce, dogged fighters of Spain as she was four hundred years ago could have cut this path. Even then, when men thought little of life or of accomplishing the impossible, the Trail stood forth as a great achievement, every mile of which had cost the lives of men.

For a time, the adventurers stared in silence at the brown line athwart the green, the sign and seal of an empire long passed away. Then Pinto grounded the montaria at the edge of the bank, and, after all of the party had disembarked with their scanty equipment, pulled the boat, with Hen's help, back of a screen of tangled vines, marked by a slender assai-palm, until it was completely, hidden from sight.

"If we are successful," remarked Professor Ditson, "we'll never see that boat again. If we are driven back along this trail, it may save our lives."

There was a silence. For the first time the boys and Jud realized that their leader definitely expected perils other than those ever present from the wild creatures that guarded the beautiful, treacherous, mysterious forests of this southern continent.

"Are the Injuns down here dangerous?" inquired Jud, at last.

"The personal habits of some of them do not commend themselves even to the most broad-minded investigators," returned the professor, precisely.

"Such as—" questioned Jud, again.

"Well," replied the scientist, slowly, "for one thing, the wild tribes of this part of the Amazon basin invariably eat any captives they make. Then—"

"That's enough," broke in Jud. "After

I've been eaten I don't care what they do next. What might be the names of these gentlemen?"

"The Mayas, I think, are the tribe we shall be most likely to meet," said Professor Ditson, reflectively. "They have no fixed homes, but wander through the forest, guiding themselves by the sun, and sleep in the tree-tops like monkeys wherever they happen to be when night comes. They hunt men, red, white, or black," he went on; "yet, if Indian traditions can be depended upon, we do not need to be afraid of them so long as we keep to the Trail."

"How's that?" inquired Will, intensely interested.

"Every tribe which refers to the Trail," the scientist informed them, "speaks of a custom called the 'Truce of the Trail,' under which travelers along that road are safe from attack."

"Does that there truce," interposed Jud, "take in white men, or is it only for redskins?"

"That," returned the professor, "is not certain. Some say yes, some say no."

"The question is," murmured Jud, "what do the Mayas say?"

"If we pass the Trail in safety," went on Professor Ditson, "we still may expect trouble from Dawson after we get into the Peruvian highlands. He has great influence with a band of Indian outlaws who call themselves the Miranhas, or Killers, and may persuade them to ambush us in order to secure the map."

"I sure am lookin' forward to this pleasure-trip of ours," confided Jud to Will.

During the first day along the trail, Will, who was next to Pinto, tried to pass away the time by learning a few words of Mundurucu. His first lessons in that language, however, were somewhat discouraging, since the dialects of the South American Indians contain perhaps more syllables to a word than any other language on earth.

"Pinto," he began, "I'll point to things, and you tell me what they are in Indian, and keep on saying it over and over until I learn it."

"All right," agreed the Mundurucu.

"Professor Pinto," went on Will solemnly, pointing to his hand, "what's that?"

"In-tee-ti-pix-tee-e-toke-kee-kee-tay-gaw," clattered Pinto, in a breath.

"Hey, hold up there," said Will. "Try it in low."

Half an hour later found him still working on that single word.

"Whew!" he remarked when he finally had it memorized, "I've heard it takes eight years to learn Eskimo. It's liable to take me eighty before I can talk Mundurucu. What about this one?" he went on, undiscouraged, pointing to a curious tree with a mahogany-red bark—which, if he had but known it, was a stranger whose seeds had in some way drifted down from much farther north.

"E-lit-ta-pix-tee-e-fa-cho-to-kee-not-e," said Pinto, slowly and distinctly.

For fifteen minutes Will wrestled with this new word.

"Do you know what he said?" at last interrupted Professor Ditson, who had been listening to the lesson.

"He gave me the name for that tree, did n't he?" returned Will, a little peevishly.

"Not at all," said the scientist. "He simply said, 'I don't know.'"

"Not so blame simply, either," murmured Jud, who had also been following the lesson.

"Our own language is full of similar mistakes imported from native dialects," lectured Professor Ditson. "'Kangaroo' simply means 'I don't know' in Bushman; so do 'mosquito' and 'quinine' and 'cockatoo' in different Indian languages."

"Well," said Will, "I'm going to pass up Mundurucu. Here I've spent the better part of an hour in learning two words—and one of them is n't right."

"It's a gift, my boy," said Jud, patronizingly. "As for myself, I once learned three Indian languages, Apache, Comanche, an' Sioux, in less than a month."

"Indeed!" broke in Professor Ditson, cuttingly. "You surprise me. Won't you favor me with a few sentences in Apache?"

"Surely," returned Jud, generously. "Ask

me anything you like in Apache, an' I'll be glad to answer it in the same language."

The appearance of a small pond ahead put a stop to further adventure in linguistics, since Pinto had promised to catch some fish from the next water they met. As they came to the shore, suddenly, before Jud's astonished eyes, a fish about a foot long thrust its head out of the dark water, opened its mouth, and breathed like any mammal. A moment later it meowed like a cat, growled like a dog, and then went under.

"I'll never dare tell 'em about this in Cornwall," exclaimed Jud, earnestly, as the talented fish disappeared. "They'd think I was exaggeratin', an' that's one thing I never do. This trip," he went on reflectively, "is liable to make me believe blame near anything."

It was Professor Ditson who told them that the strange fish was a lung-fish and was a link between the fishes and the reptiles.

A little later, Pinto, with a length of flexible palm-fiber, noosed a garpike, that strange reresentative of the oldest family of fishes

left on earth, and another link with the reptiles. Its vertebræ had ball-and-socket joints
like the spine of a snake, and, unlike any
other fish, it could move its head independ-
ently of its body. Armored scales arranged
in diagonal rows ran down its back, being
fastened to each other by a system of hooks,
instead of lapping over each other like the
scales of other fishes. This armor was of
such flinty hardness that Pinto struck a spark
from it with his steel, and actually lighted
from its own scales the fire on which the fish
was cooked.

By this pond grew a great orchid with
thirty-one flower-stems, on one of which
Will counted over a thousand beautiful pearl-
and-gold blossoms. Near the water, too, were
many varieties of tropical birds flaming
through the trees. Among them were flocks
of paraquets colored green and blue and red;
little honey-creepers with black, purple, and
turquoise plumage and brilliant scarlet feet;
and exquisite tiny tanagers like clusters of
jewels with their lilac throats, turquoise
breasts, topaz crowns, and purple-black backs

shading into ruby red. These were all search-
ing for insects, while among the blossoms
whirred dainty little humming-birds of the
variety known as "wood-stars." Then there
were blood-red macaws with blue-and-gold
wings, and lustrous green-black toucans with
white throats, red-and-yellow tail-coverts,
and huge black-and-yellow bills.

For the next few days the treasure-hunters followed the narrow, hard-beaten path
through stretches of dark jungle and thorny
thickets, or found themselves skirting lonely
lakes hidden in the very heart of the virgin
forest. Everywhere the Trail was omniously
clear and hard-trodden. Sometimes they all
had that strange knowledge that they were
being watched, which human beings who live
in the open acquire as well as the wild folk.

At last there came a day when the supplies
had run so low that it became necessary for
Pinto to do some hunting. Will went with
him, and together they silently and cautiously
followed one of the many little paths that at
irregular intervals branched off from the main
trail. This one was so hidden by vines and

creepers that it seemed improbable that any
one had used it for a long period of time.   It
led the hunters into one of the patches of open
country sometimes found in the forests of the
Amazon. This particular one was fringed
with great trees and crossed by another path
nearly parallel to the one they were following.

Near the center of the clearing, Pinto
managed to shoot two curassows, huge, plump
birds which looked and tasted much like tur-
keys. Leaving these with his companion, the
Indian pushed on ahead for more. Suddenly
he reappeared among the trees, and Will noticed as he hurried toward him, that his copper-
colored face showed gray and drawn, while
beads of sweat stood out on his forehead. As
he joined the boy, Pinto placed his finger on
his lips with a look of ghastly terror and led
Will into the deepest part of a near-by thicket.
From there, though hidden from sight, they
had a view through the close-set bushes of the
other path. Suddenly, from far down that
trail, sounded a faint, but regular, clicking
noise. As it became louder and louder, rising and falling in a regular cadence, Pinto

slipped like a snake deeper into the long jungle-grass.

"Lie still for your life," he whispered in Will's ear, so faintly that the boy could scarcely make out the words. Then, in an instant, from out of the jungle not twenty feet away there strode along the dim path a figure of nightmare horror—that of a tall naked man, with gaunt and fleshless arms and legs, great knobs of bone marking his knee and elbow-joints. His sunken body was painted black, with every bone outlined in a chalky white, so that he seemed a living, walking skeleton.

Around the black and wasted neck, wrinkled like that of a mummy, hung a long string of small bones which, with a thrill of horror, the boy recognized by their nails as those of human fingers. It was these, striking together, which made the clicking noise that Will had heard. The face of the horror was painted black, except the lips and chin, which showed blood-red, while out of the holes at the corners of the lower lip protruded curved, gleaming peccary-tusks. These ornaments gave an indescribably brutish appearance to the countenance that they ornamented, while above them two snaky black eyes with an expression of implacable cruelty glittered like crumbs of glass from under overhanging brows. Like a specter, the shape disappeared among the shadows; but it was followed by another and another and another, until a long procession of terrible figures had passed.

As the ill-omened clicking died away in the distance Will sprang to his feet.

"No!" hissed the Indian. "Our only chance of life is to lie quiet. That is a Maya war-party on a man-hunt!"

"They'll meet the others on the Trail," whispered Will.

"Six men can't do any more against fifty than two," returned Pinto, practically. "We'll only throw away our lives and not save theirs."

"Stay if you want," returned the boy; "I'll live or die with them!" and he sped back at full speed along the path over which they had come. Just before he reached the Trail he looked back—and there was Pinto at his shoulder.

"Very foolish," the latter muttered, "but— I come too."

Down the Trail the two hurried, and, rounding a bend, burst in suddenly upon the rest of the party lying in the shade of the overhanging trees awaiting their return.

"Mayas! Mayas!" gasped Pinto.

As he spoke, far down the Trail from around a curve sounded the faint, ominous clicking which the two hunters had heard before.

It was then that the old scientist showed that he deserved the right to lead which he claimed.

"Stand still!" he said sternly to Pinto, as the latter seemed inclined to bolt down the Trail away from the fatal sound. "Put up your gun!" he ordered Jud; "the Truce is our only chance."

Then, with quick, decisive commands, he lined the party up so that no part of the body of any one of them extended beyond the surface of the Trail, and yet a space was left wide

enough to allow any others using the path to
pass.   At the head of the line he placed the
two Indians, Joe and Pinto, so that the Mayas
might note the presence in the party of members of their own race.

"Show the peace sign," he snapped sharply
to Joe, who led the line.   "Brace up!" he
went on, slapping Pinto sharply on his bare
back; "don't look so scared.   No matter what
they do," he said, turning to the rest of the
company, "don't leave the Trail for a second
or make any kind of attack on them.   They
will probably try to make us break the Truce
of the Trail.   If any of us do, we are all lost."

"My peace sign," muttered Jud, grimly,
"will be an automatic in one hand an' this
little toothpick in the other," and he opened
the five-inch blade of the jack-knife with
which he had killed old Three Toes, the
grizzly, as already chronicled in "The Blue
Pearl."   "If I 'm goin' to be eaten," he went
on, "there 'll be eighteen Mayas that ain't
goin' to have any appetite for the meal"; and
he shifted the single clip of cartridges re-

maining, so that he could feed them into the automatic if it came to a last stand.

All further conversation was ended by the appearance of the same horrible apparition which had so terrified Pinto a short time before. As the gaunt painted skeleton of the first Maya showed against the green background, surmounted by the black and blood-red face with the grinning tusks and implacable eyes, an involuntary gasp went up from the whole waiting party. Jud slipped the safety-catch from his revolver; Pinto's face looked as if suddenly powdered with ashes; Will's hands stole to the hatchet at his belt; while, down at the end of the line, Hen Pine gripped his heavy machete until his great muscles stood out like iron bands. Two of the party alone showed no sign of any emotion: Joe, the descendant of a long line of of proud Chippewa chiefs, disdainfully stretched out both empty hands palms up in the peace-sign; while Professor Ditson's calm face seemed to show only the mild interest of a scientist.

As the leading Maya caught sight of the waiting line, he slowed his swift stride and the war-party crept up close and closer. Then came the tense moment which would decide whether the Truce was to hold. As the grim hunters moved up, there was no sign on the face of any of them of any acceptance of the peace which Joe had offered. With short, gliding steps, they made a complete circle around the little party, closing up until their menacing, fearful faces were less than a foot away and the reek of their naked bodies was like the hot taint of jaguars of the jungle in the nostrils of the waiting six. In their left hands they carried bows and quivers of fiercely fanged arrows gummed with fatal venom, while from their belts swung curved, saw-toothed knives and short, heavy clubs, the heads of which were studded with alligators' teeth.

As the Mayas came closer, the waiting line wavered involuntarily before the terrible menace of their hating, hateful faces. The Mundurucu especially, although no coward, had been taught from earliest childhood to dread these man-eaters, the Mayas. It was Professor Ditson who noticed that, in spite of their menacing approach, not a single warrior had as yet gripped a weapon.

"Steady, Pinto, steady all," he said calmly, "They're trying to stampede us. If one of you leaves the Trail, we're all dead men."

He spoke just in time, for already Pinto was looking longingly toward the refuge of the forest, forgetting that the woodcraft of those hunters of men was superior even to his own. Perhaps even Professor Ditson's voice would not have stopped him if it had not been for a sudden happening.

As the leader of the Mayas half-circled around Joe, the latter turned to face him, still holding out his arms. The motion flung open his flannel shirt, unbuttoned to the waist, and showed, tattooed red on his brown skin, the curling, twisted totem-mark of intertwined serpents by which Joe had claimed the right of his blood in the lodge of the Great Chief during the quest of the Blue Pearl. As the Maya caught sight of this sign he stopped in his tracks. Little by little the

menace died out of his fierce eyes, and, as if
drawn by a magnet, he crept in closer and
closer with outstretched neck, staring at the
tattoo marks which wound down and around
Joe's waist.   Then, with a sudden gesture, he
swept aside the ghastly necklace that he wore.
There, outlined against his fleshless chest
just over his heart, showed a similar
emblem—crimson inter-twining serpents facing in opposite directions, with gaping
mouths like those of which the totem-pole was
made which towered before the lodge of the
Great Chief in far-away Akotan.   The Maya
chief stood motionless for a moment.   Then
he stretched both hands out toward Joe, palms
up, and stood as if waiting.

"Put your hands in his, boy," hissed Jud,
from down the line; "he's waitin' for the
brotherhood sign."

Without a word, Joe clasped hands with
the Maya chief, and for an instant the two
looked into each other's eyes, the spectral
cannibal and the lithe son of a French trapper
and a Chippewa princess.   Then, disengag-

ing his right hand, the Maya fumbled at his belt and suddenly stretched out toward Joe the supple, beautiful tanned skin of a snake, such as but one of the party had ever seen before. It was long and narrow and of a flashing golden-yellow, thickly flecked with tiny red-brown spots. This he wound around the boy's neck, so that it swung gleaming against his gray flannel shirt. Once again with outstretched hands the strange figure stood as if waiting, encircled the while by fierce, impassive faces with tusks gleaming horribly against blood-red jaws, and white painted bodies showing like ghosts against the green of the forest.

"Give him your tie," dictated Jud. "Don't you know blood-brothers have to exchange presents?"

Joe hesitated. He had a weakness, perhaps inherited from both sides of his family, for neckties of the most barbaric colors. The one that he was wearing was one of Cornwall's best and brightest, a brilliant green-and-purple creation which had cost him a whole dollar at White Wilcox's store. To give it up would leave him tieless in a great wilderness.

"Hurry!" muttered Professor Ditson, as the Maya chief began to lower his outstretched hands.

Thus urged, the boy reluctantly pulled a foot of glimmering silk from his neck, and the next instant the most brilliant tie that ever graced Mr. Wilcox's emporium was gleaming against the gray-white of a necklace of human bones.

The Maya received the enforced present with a grunt of undisguised pleasure, and, raising both hands above his head with palms outstretched, faced his waiting band and began a crooning song filled with strange minor cadences. One by one his men took up the strain, and, led by him, filed away from the trail like ghosts going back to their graves. As the clicking of their necklaces and the notes of their chant sounded faint and fainter and at last died away in the green tangle of the jungle, a long sigh of relief came unconsciously from every member of the expedition. It was Jud who first broke the silence.

"I 've always heard," he said, "that Injuns north, south, east, an' west belonged to the four main totems, the Bear, the Wolf, the Snake, an' the Eagle, but I never believed it before to-day. That old tattoo-mark, boy," he went on, turning to Joe, "certainly came in right handy."

"He gone off with my good tie," returned Joe, sorrowfully.

"And a good job, too, I call it," remarked Will, who had never approved his friend's taste in neckwear.

It was the Maya's present which most interested Pinto and Professor Ditson. The Mundurucu Indian sidled up close to Joe and stared at the glittering skin with all his eyes, but without attempting to touch it.

"It 's the sacred snake that in the old days only kings and gods could wear," he murmured.

"He 's right," said Professor Ditson, raising the gleaming, golden skin reverently from Joe's neck. "It's the skin of the Yellow Snake which the Aztecs used to wind around the forehead of Atapetl, their terrible goddess of war. Only her priests knew where to find these snakes, and it was death for any one else even to look at the skin except at the annual sacrifices of the goddess. This one," he went on, "will be a safe-conduct for the whole party all the way to Peru—and ought to be a lesson to you," he continued severely, turning to Jud, "never to speak against snakes again."

CHAPTER VIII

THE MAN-EATERS

FIVE days later they came to a great lake which seemed to stretch away through the depths of the forest interminably, with the trail following its winding shores.

At the first sight of the water shining in the sunlight, Pinto showed signs of great uneasiness.

"This must be the Lake of the Man-eaters," he said to Professor Ditson. "I have heard the wise men of the tribe speak of it many times. All the animals around it are eaters of men. See, perhaps there be some of their tracks now!" and he pointed to where there showed in the soft sand what looked like the paw-prints of a huge cat.

"Pinto," said the professor, severely, "I'm ashamed of you! The sight of those Mayas has made your mind run on man-eaters.

Don't you know a puma's track when you see them, and don't you know that a puma never attacks a man?"

"'The perfesser's right for once," chimed in Jud. "That's the track of what we call a mountain-lion or panther up north, an' they don't never hurt nobody."

Pinto was still unconvinced. "Perhaps they do here," he insisted.

"You come along with me," returned Professor Ditson. "We'll explore this lake a bit before dark." And, followed by all of the party except Will and Jud, whose turn it was to make camp, he disappeared around a bend in the shore.

The two who were left behind soon found a high, sandy bank where they cleared a space and started a small fire. Just in front of them was a tiny bay, connected with the lake by a narrow channel edged by lines of waving ferns, while a little beach of white sand curved away to the water in front of the camp-site.

"Here is where Judson Adams, Esquire, takes a bath," suddenly announced the old trapper, producing a couple of cakes of tree-soap, which he had picked along the trail, and slipping out of his clothes like an eel.

"Pinto said never to go into strange water," warned Will.

"Pooh," said Jud. "He was talkin' about rivers where them murderin' catfish an 'anacondas hide. This pool ain't ten feet across an' there's nothin' in it except a few stray minnies"; and he pointed out to Will a little school of short, deep-bodied fish which looked something like the sunfish which the boys used to catch along the edges of Cream Hill Pond. Otherwise no living creature showed in the clear water, nor could be concealed along the bright, pebbly bottom.

"Better not," warned Will again. "This ain't your country, Jud. Pinto seemed to know what he was talking about. Let's wait until the professor gets back."

"Pinto will never win any Carnegie medals, an' I guess I can take a bath without gettin' permission from the perfesser," returned Jud, obstinately. "However," he went on, "just to show you that the old man never takes any chances, I 'll poke a stick around in this pool to drive out the devil-fish that may be hidin' here."

Nothing happened as the old man prodded the water with a long branch cut from a near-by tree, except that the motion of the stick seemed to attract more and more of the chubby fish which he had first seen from the outer channel into the pool.

"Gee," remarked Jud, "but those fish are tame! I 'll bet if I had a hook an' line I could flick out a dozen. Better come in with me, Bill," he went on. "I promised your family that I 'd see that you boys took plenty of baths an' kept your hair brushed all through this trip."

"I 'll wait till the boss comes back," said Will, laughingly.

That was enough for Jud.

"I 'm my own boss!" he remarked indignantly, and waded in with a cake of tree-grown soap clenched tightly in one hand.

His first step took him well above his knees. There was a swirl and a flash from the center of the pool, and in an instant the whole surface was alive with a furious rush of the short, deep-bodied fish toward Jud. As they approached, the old man noticed uneasily their staring, malignant eyes, and that they had projecting, gaping lower jaws, thickly set with razor-edged, triangular teeth.

Suddenly the whole school were upon him, crowding into the shallow water where he stood and snapping at his bare legs like mad dogs. Before he could stir, two of them had bitten pieces of flesh out of the calves of both of his legs. As the blood from their bites touched the surface of the pool, the fish seemed to go entirely mad, snapping their fierce jaws frantically and even springing clear of the water, like trout leaping at a fly.

If they had not been so numerous that they jostled each other, or if Jud had not been quicker than most men twenty years younger, he would have been terribly mutilated. As it was, when he finally reached the safety of the bank, the water which he had just left boiled and bubbled like a caldron, and two of the fish followed him so closely that they landed, flapping, snapping, and squealing, far up on the white sand.

When Will approached them, the stranded fish tried to spring at him, clicking their jaws with impotent, savage fury. A moment later, as he tried to hold one of them down with a stick, it drove its keen wedge-shaped teeth clear through the hard wood. When the rest of the party came back, they found Jud and Will staring as if fascinated at the desperate, raging dwellers of the pool.

"I told you strange water not safe," said Pinto, as Professor Ditson skilfully bandaged Jud's legs with a dressing of sphagnum moss and the thick red sap of the dragon's-blood tree. "Look," and he showed Will that a joint of one of his fingers was missing. "Cannibal-fish more dangerous than anaconda or piraiba. They kill tiger and eat up alligator if it get wounded. Once," he went on, "white man ride a mule across river where these fish live. They bit mule and he threw man off into the river. When I got there an hour later only skeleton left of mule. Man's clothes lie at bottom of river, but only bones inside. You wait a little. I pay them well." And he disappeared into the woods.

Professor Ditson corroborated the Indian.

"They are undoubtedly the fiercest and most dangerous fish that swim," he said. "If the water is disturbed, it arouses them, and the taste or smell of blood seems to drive them mad."

By the time Jud was patched up, Pinto came back trailing behind him a long length of liana, from either end of which oozed a white liquid. This vine he pounded between two stones and threw into the pool. A minute later the water was milky from the flowing juice, and before long was filled with floating, motionless piranhas stupefied by the poisonous sap. Pinto fished out several with a long stick, and breaking their necks, wrapped them in balls of blue clay which he found along the shore, and, first making air-holes, set them to bake in the hot coals of the fire. When at last a smell of roast fish went up from the midst of the fire, Pinto pulled each ball out and broke the hard surface with light taps of a stick. The skin and scales came off with the clay. Opening the fish carefully, he cleaned it, leaving nothing but the savory white baked meat, which tasted and looked almost exactly like black bass. Jud avenged himself by eating seven.

Toward the end of the afternoon, Professor Amandus Ditson left the rest of the party reclining in that state of comfort and satisfaction which comes after a good meal. Each day the professor devoted all of his spare time toward realizing the greatest ambition of his life, to wit, the acquirement of one full-grown, able-bodied bushmaster. To-day armed with nothing more dangerous than a long crotched stick, he strolled along the trail, leaving it occasionally to search every mound or hillock which showed above the flat level of the jungle, since in such places this king of the pit-vipers is most apt to be found. Two hundred yards away from the camp, the trail took a turn, following the curved shore of the great lake, and in a few minutes the scientist was entirely out of sight or sound of the rest of the party. At last, finding nothing in-

land he turned his steps toward the lake itself.   On some bare spaces showing between
the trail and the edge of the water, he saw
more of the puma-tracks like those which
Pinto had pointed out earlier in the day.   Remembering the Indian's fear the scientist
smiled as he examined the fresh prints of big
pads and long claws.

"Harmless as tomcats," he muttered to
himself.

A moment later something happened which
upset both the professor and his theories.   As
he straightened up, a hundred pounds of
puma landed upon him.   The legend of the
lake, as far as pumas were concerned, was
evidently correct.   Harmless to man in other
places, here, it seemed, the great cat stalked
men as if they were deer.   This one intended
to sink the curved claws of her forepaws in
the professor's shoulders, and, with her teeth
at his throat, to rake his body with the terrible
downward, slashing strokes of the catamount
clan.   Fortunately for himself, he had half-
turned at the sound which her sudden spring
made among the bushes.   Instead of catching

his throat, the panther's fanged jaws closed on the upper part of his left arm, while her forepaws gripped his shoulders, which were protected by a khaki coat and flannel shirt. Professor Ditson promptly caught the animal's throat with his sinewy right hand and held the great beast off at arm's length, thus keeping his body beyond the range of the deadly sickle-like hind claws. For a moment the puma's luminous gooseberry green eyes stared into his, and he could see the soft white of her under parts and the long, tawny tail which is the hall-mark of her family. As he sank his steel-strong fingers deeper into the great brute's throat, Professor Ditson abandoned all hope of life, for no unarmed man can hope to cope successfully with any of the great carnivora.

"A dozen zoölogists have lied in print!" he murmured to himself, indignantly.

Even as he spoke, he tried to wrench his left arm free. He immediately found, however, that it was impossible to pull it straight out from between the keen teeth. Sinking his fingers deeper into the puma's throat, he

squeezed it suddenly with all of his strength.
Involuntarily, as the wind was shut off from
her lungs, the gripping jaws relaxed enough
to allow the scientist to pull his arm through
them for a few inches sidewise. Again the
puma caught the moving arm, a few inches
lower down. Again, as the man gripped her
throat afresh, she relaxed her hold, and he
gained an inch or so before the sharp teeth
clamped tight again. Inch by inch, the professor worked the full length of his arm
through the fierce jaws which, in spite of
the khaki sleeve and thick shirt beneath,
pierced and crushed terribly the tense muscles of his arm.

Throughout the struggle the tawny beast
kept up a continual grunting, choking snarl,
while the man fought in utter silence. At last
the whole length of the professor's left arm
had been dragged through, until only his hand
itself was in the mouth of the puma. Shoving
it down her hot gullet, he gripped the base of
her tongue so chokingly that the struggling
panther was unable to close her jaws, and, for
the first time during the fight, the professor

was free from the pain of her piercing teeth.

In a desperate struggle to release the grip which was shutting off her breath, the puma lurched over and fell full length on her back in the loose sand, dragging the man down with her, and the professor found himself with his left hand deep in her gullet, his right hand still clutching the beast's throat desperately, while his knees, with the weight of his body back of them, pressed full against her ribs on each side. As they struck the ground he sank his elbows into the armpits of the puma beneath him, spreading her front legs and pinning them down, so that her frantic claws could reach inward only enough to rip his coat, without wounding the flesh beneath. Once on the ground, the panther struggled fiercely, pitching and bucking in an effort to release herself from the man's weight so that she could be in a position to make use of the curved scimitars with which all four of her paws were armed. The loose sand shifted and gave her no purchase.

As they fought, Professor Ditson felt his strength leaving him with the blood that flowed from his gashed and mangled arm. Raising himself a little, he surged down with both knees and felt a rib snap under his weight and the struggling body relax a trifle. For the first time he dared hope to do what no man had done since the cavemen contended with their foes among the beast-folk, and to his surprise noted that he was beginning to take a certain grim pleasure in the combat. The fury of the fight had pierced through the veneer of education and culture, and Professor Amandus Ditson, the holder of degrees from half a dozen learned universities, battled for his life that day with a beast of the forest with all the desperation and fierce joy which any of his prehistoric forebears might have felt a hundred thousand years ago.

It had become a question as to which would give up first—the man or the beast. Fighting off the waves of blackness which seemed to surge up and up until they threatened to close over his head, he fought desperately with clutching hands and driving knees, under which the thin ribs of the puma snapped like dry branches, until at last, with a long, con-

vulsive shudder, the great cat stopped breathing.   Even as he felt the tense body relax and
become motionless under his grip, the blackness closed over his head.

There the rest of the party, alarmed by his
long absence, found him an hour later. His
gaunt body was stretched out on the dead
panther and his right hand was sunk in the
long fur, while his left hand and arm were
buried to the elbow in the fierce gaping mouth
and his bowed knees still pinned the great
cat down. Around the dead beast and the
unconscious man sat four black vultures.
Thrusting forward from time to time their
naked, red, hooded heads, they seemed about
to begin their feast when the rescuing party
arrived. With his face hidden in the panther's
tawny fur, Professor Ditson seemed as dead
as the beast that lay beneath him. It was
not until Hen had pried his fingers away from
the puma's throat and carefully drawn his
gashed hand from the beast's gullet that his
eyes flickered open and his gaunt chest strained
with a long, labored breath.

"I was wrong," were his first words. "The

Felis concolor does occasionally attack man. I 'll make a note of it," he went on weakly, "in the next edition of my zoölogy."

"I was wrong, too," burst out Jud, pressing close up to the exhausted scientist and clasping his uninjured hand in both of his. "I thought you were nothin' but a perfesser, but I want to say right here an' now that you 're a *man.*"

The danger, however, was not yet over. The scratches and bites of a panther or a jaguar, like those of a lion or tiger, almost invariably cause death from blood-poisoning if not immediately treated. Under Professor Ditson's half-whispered directions, they stripped off his clothes, washed away the blood and dirt with clear water, and then, using the little surgical kit which he always wore at his belt, injected a solution of iodine into every scratch and tooth-mark.

"It is necessary," said the scientist, gritting his teeth as the stinging liquid smarted and burned like fire, "but I do not believe that life itself is worth so much suffering."

The rest of the party, however, did not

agree with this perhaps hasty opinion, and persisted in their treatment until every puncture was properly sterilized. Then, bandaged with great handfuls of cool sphagnum moss and attended by the faithful Hen Pine, the professor slept the clock around. While he was asleep, Will and Pinto slipped away together to see if they could not bring back a plump curassow from which to make broth for him when he finally woke up; while Jud and Joe, with similar good intentions, scoured the jungle for the best-flavored fruits they might find.

Will and his companion found the birds scarce although they slipped through the jungle like shadows. As they penetrated deeper among the trees they were careful to walk so that their shadows fell directly behind them, which meant that they were walking in a straight line, along which they could return by observing the same precaution. As they reached a tiny grove of wild oranges, Will's quick eye caught sight of something which gleamed white against the dark trunks, and the two went over to investigate. There they saw a grisly sight. Coiled in a perfect circle were the bones of an anaconda some fifteen feet in length. Every vertebra and rib, and even the small bones of the head and the formidable, recurved teeth, were perfect, while in all the great skeleton there was not a fragment of flesh nor a scale of the skin remaining. Strangest of all, inclosed by the ribs of the snake was the crushed skeleton of a large monkey, which likewise had been cleaned and polished beyond the skill of any human anatomist or taxidermist. Some terrible foe had attacked the great snake while lying helpless and torpid after its heavy meal and had literally devoured it alive. The face of the Indian was very grave as he looked at the gleaming bones before him, and he stared carefully through the adjoining thickets before speaking.

"Puma bad man-eater," he said at last; "cannibal-fish worse; but anicton most dangerous of all. He eat same as fire eats. He kill jaguar, sucurucu, bushmaster, alligator,

Indian, white man. He afraid of nothing."

"What is the anicton?" inquired Will, frightened in spite of himself.

Even as he spoke, from far beyond in the jungle came a strange, rustling whisper which seemed to creep along the ground and pass on and on through the woods like the hiss of spreading flames.

"Come," said the Indian, briefly, "I show you." And he led Will farther out into the jungle through which the menacing whisper seemed to hurry to meet them.

Soon small flocks of plain-colored birds could be seen flying low, with excited twitterings, evidently following the course of some unseen objects on the ground. Then there came a rustling through the underbrush, and, in headlong flight, an army of little animals, reptiles, and insects dashed through the jungle. Long brown wood-rats scuttled past, tiny jumping-mice leaped through the air, guiding themselves with their long tails, while here and there centipedes, small snakes, and a multitude of other living creatures sped through the brush as if fleeing before a forest fire.

Suddenly, through a corner of the jungle thrust the van of a vast army of black ants. Through the woods they moved in lines and regiments and divisions, while little companies deployed here and there on each side of the main guard. Like a stream of dark lava, the army flowed swiftly over the ground. As with human armies, this one was made up of different kinds of soldiers, all of whom had different duties to perform. Most numerous of all were the eyeless workers, about half an inch in length, armed with short, but keen, cutting mandibles. These acted as carriers and laborers and reserves, and, although blind, were formidable by reason of their numbers. Larger than the workers, measuring a full inch in length, were the soldiers, with enormous square heads and mandibles pointed and curved like pairs of ice-tongs. These soldiers would drive in each mandible alternately until they met in the body of their victim, and when they met they held.

Even if the body of the ants was torn away, the curved clinging jaws still clinched and bit. With the soldiers came companies of butchers, whose jaws had serrated teeth which sheared and cut through flesh and muscle like steel saws. Besides these, there were laborers and reserve soldiers by the million.

Pinto told Will that a large ant-army would take twenty-four hours to pass a given point even when traveling at full speed. As they watched this army, Will saw an exhibition of what it could do. A large agouti in fleeing before them had in some way caught its leg in a tangle of vines and, squealing in terror, tried in vain to escape. Before it could release itself, the rush of the army was upon it, and it disappeared under a black wave of biting, stinging ants, which methodically cut up and carried off every fragment of the animal's flesh, and passed on, leaving behind only a picked skeleton.

As Will watched this hurrying, resistless multitude, although well beyond the path of its advance, he felt a kind of terror, and was relieved when the Mundurucu started back for camp.

"Nothing that lives," said Pinto, as they turned toward the trail, "can stand against the black army."

The next day Jud and Joe joined in the hunt, leaving Hen to nurse the professor. Following a deer trail back from the shore, they came to a patch of swampy woods a mile from the lake. There Will discovered a mound some five feet high made of rushes, rotting moss, leaves, and mold.

"Is that a nest of ants?" he called to the Indian, pointing out to him the symmetrical hillock.

Pinto's face lighted up.

"No," he said, "that a nest of eggs. We dig it out, have good supper to-night."

"It must be some bird," exclaimed Jud, hurrying up, "to make a nest like that. Probably one of them South American ostriches— hey, Pinto?"

"You 'll see," was all that the Indian would say as he began to dig into the soft, spongy mass. The rest of the party followed his example. By the time they had reached the center of the mound, digging with sticks and bare hands, the matted, rotting vegetation felt warm to the touch, and this heat increased as they approached the base of the nest. Down at the very bottom of the mound, arranged in a circle on a bed of moss, they found no fewer than twenty-four white eggs as large as those of a duck, but round and covered with a tough, parchment-like shell.

Pinto hurriedly pouched them all in a netted game-bag which he had made for himself out of palm-fiber.

"Want to see bird that laid those eggs?" he asked Jud.

"I sure would," returned the old trapper. "Any fowl that builds a five-foot incubator like that must be worth seein'."

"Rub two eggs together and she come," directed Pinto, holding out his bag to Jud.

Following the Indian's suggestion, Jud unsuspectingly rubbed two of the eggs against each other. They made a curious, penetrating, grating noise, like the squeal of chalk on a blackboard.

Hardly had the sound died away, when from out of a near-by wet thicket there came a roaring bellow that shook the very ground they stood on, and suddenly the air was filled with the sweet sickly scent of musk. Jud turned as if stung by a fire-ant, to see a pair of green eyes glaring at him above the jaws of a great alligator which had been lurking in the darkness of the jungle. As it lay there like an enormous lizard, the dark gray of its armored hide hardly showed against the shadows. On each side of the fore part of the upper jaw, two cone-shaped tusks showed white as polished ivory, fitting into sockets in the lower jaw. Even as Jud looked, the upper jaw of the vast saurian was raised straight up, showing the blood-red lining of the mouth gaping open fully three feet. Then, with a roar like distant thunder, the great reptile raised its body, as big as that of a horse, upon its short, squat legs, and rushed through the brush at Jud with a squattering gait, which, however, carried it over the ground at a tremendous rate of speed for a creature eighteen feet long.

It was Jud's first experience with an alligator, and with a yell he ran down the slope like a race-horse. Unfortunately for him, on a straight line downhill an alligator can run faster than a man, and this one began to overtake him rapidly. As he glanced back, the grinning jaws seemed right at his shoulder.

"Dodge him! Dodge him!" yelled Pinto.

At first, Jud paid no attention, but ran straight as a deer will sometimes run between the rails to its death before a locomotive when one bound to the side would save it. At last, as Will and Joe also began to shout the same words over and over again, the idea penetrated Jud's bewildered brain and he sprang to one side and doubled on his trail. His pursuer, however, specialized in doubling itself. Unable to turn rapidly on account of its great length, and seeing its prey escaping, the alligator curved its body and the long serrated tail swung over the ground like a scythe. The extreme end of it caught Jud just above the ankles and swept him off his feet, standing him on his head in a thorn-bush from which he was rescued by Pinto and Will, who had followed close behind. The alligator made no further attempt at pursuit, but quickly disappeared in the depths of a marshy thicket.

"Whew!" said Jud, exhausted, sitting down on a fallen log and mopping his steaming face. "That was certainly a funny joke, Mr. Pinto. About one more of those an' you won't go any further on this trip. You'll stay right here—underground."

The Mundurucu was very apologetic, explaining that he had not intended to do anything worse than startle the old man, while Will and Joe interceded for him.

"He only wanted to see you run," said the latter, slyly. "Nobody can run like Jud when he's scared."

"No, boy," objected the old trapper, "I was n't exactly scared. Startled is the right word. It would startle anybody to have a monstrophalus alligator rush out of nowhere an' try to swallow him."

"Certainly it would," agreed Will, gravely.

"Anybody could see that you were n't scared, you looked so noble when you ran."

Peace thus being restored, the whole party returned to camp, where that night Professor Ditson, who was feeling better, gave a long discourse on the difference between crocodiles, alligators, and caymans.

"If that had been a crocodile," he explained "you would n't be here now. There 's one species found in South America, and it 's far faster than any alligator. Look out for it."

"I most certainly will," murmured Jud.

That night at supper, Pinto proceeded to roast in the hot coals the whole clutch of alligator eggs except the two which Jud had dropped in his excitement. For the first time in a long life, the old trapper refused the food set before him.

"I 've et monkeys an' dragons an' cannibalfish without a murmur," he said, "but I draw the line at alligator's eggs. They may taste all right, but when I think of their dear old mother an' how she took to me, I 'm just sentimental enough to pass 'em up."

CHAPTER IX

THE PIT

FOR several days the treasure-hunters made their camp near the shores of the great lake, waiting for the slow healing of Professor Ditson's wounds. Here and there, through open spaces in the forest, they could see the summits of mountain-ranges towering away in the distance, and realized that the long journey through the jungle was nearly over. Beyond the lake the trail stretched away along the slopes of the foot-hills, with plateaus and high pampas on one side and the steaming depths of the jungle on the other.

One morning Professor Ditson felt so much better that Hen Pine, who had been acting as his special nurse, decided to start on an expedition after fresh vegetables. Shouldering his ax and beckoning to Joe, for whom the giant black had a great liking, the two struck off from the trail beyond the lake into the heart of the jungle. Before long they saw in the distance the beautiful plume-like foliage of a cabbage-palm outlined against the sky. A full seventy feet from the ground, the umbrella-like mass of leaves hung from the slim, steel-like column of the tapering trunk, buttressed by clumps of straight, tough roots, which formed a solid support to the stem of the tree extending up ten feet from the ground. It took a solid hour of chopping before the palm fell. When at last it struck the earth, Hen cut out from the heart of the tree's crown a back-load of tender green leaves folded in buds, which made a delicious salad when eaten raw and tasted like asparagus when boiled.

As they turned back, Joe saw something move in a near-by tree. Looking more closely, he noticed a crevice in the trunk, across which was stretched a dense white web. Behind this crouched a huge spider. Covered with coarse gray and reddish hairs, its ten legs had an expanse of fully seven inches. The lower part of the web was broken, and in it were entangled two small birds about the size of a field-sparrow. One of them was dead, but the other still moved feebly under the body of the monster. Picking up a long stick, Joe started to rescue the fluttering little captive.

"Look out!" shouted Hen, who was some distance away. "That's a crab-spider and mighty dangerous."

Paying no attention to the other's warning, Joe with one sweep of his stick smashed the web and, just missing the spider, freed the dying bird, so that it fell to the ground. As he whirled his stick back for another blow, the terrible arachnid sprang like a tiger through the air, landing on the upper part of Joe's bare left arm, and, with its red eyes gleaming, was about to sink its curved envenomed mandibles deep in the boy's flesh. Only the instinctive quickness of Joe's muscles, tensed and trained by many a danger, saved him. With a snap of his stick he dashed the spider into the underbrush.

"Did he get you?" shouted Hen, anxiously.

"I think not," said Joe.

"You 'd most certainly know it if he did," returned the great negro, examining the boy's arm closely. Although it was covered with loose reddish hairs from the monster, there was no sign of any wound.

"That was a close call, boy," said Hen, carefully blowing the hairs off Joe's skin. "You am goin' to be mighty discomfortable from dese ere hairs; but if he 'd done bit you, you might have died."

Hen was a true prophet. Some of the short, hard hairs became fixed in the fine creases of Joe's skin and caused an almost maddening itching which lasted for several days.

The next day, for the first time since his meeting with the puma, Professor Amandus Ditson tried walking again. His left arm was still badly swollen and inflamed and his stiffened and bruised muscles gave him intense pain when he moved, but, in spite of Hen's protests, he insisted upon limping a mile or so down the trail and back.

"If a man gives in to his body," he remarked impatiently, when Hen remonstrated with him, "he will never get anything done."

The second day he walked still farther, and the third day, accompanied by the faithful Hen, who followed him like a shadow, he covered several miles, exploring a path that ran through the jungle parallel with the trail.

"Some one's been along here lately, Boss," said Hen, pointing out freshly broken twigs and marks in the earth.

"Probably the same hunting-party that we met before," returned the professor, indifferently. "They won't—" He broke off his sentence at the sound of a little sick, wailing cry, which seemed to come from the thick jungle close at hand.

"What's that?" said Hen, sharply, raising his heavy machete.

Without answering, the scientist turned off the trail and, raising the bushes, exposed the emaciated body of a little Indian girl about four years old. A tiny slit in the side of each nostril showed her to be a member of the Araras, a friendly tribe of forest Indians akin to the Mundurucus, to whom Pinto belonged. As she looked up at Professor Ditson, her sunken face broke into a smile.

"White man!" she whispered, in the Arara dialect which both Professor Ditson and Pinto understood. Then, pointing to herself with fingers so wasted that they looked like birds' claws, she whispered her own name, "Ala," the Indian name for those gentle, beautiful little birds which Europeans have christened "wood-stars."

The stern face of the scientist softened to an expression that even Hen had never seen there before. In spite of his injured arm, it was Professor Ditson who lifted up the little girl and carried her back to the camp. There the rest of the party found them when they returned with one of the plump curassows which Pinto generally mananged to bring back from every hunt. From this, Hen Pine hurriedly made hot, nourishing broth, with which the professor slowly fed the starved child until she dropped off to sleep, holding tightly to one of his long gaunt fingers. Several hours later the little girl woke up, seeming at first much stronger, and at once began to talk in a little voice faint as the chirp of a distant cricket. From her half-whispered sentences the professor learned that her father and mother had both been killed in a foray of the Muras. Not many months after their death, Ala herself had fallen sick of one of the forest fevers so fatal to Indian children, and had been abandoned by the tribe.

In spite of her starved condition, Ala was an attractive child. Instead of the usual shallow, shiny black eyes of Indian children, hers were big and brown and fringed with long lashes, and when she smiled it was as if an inner light shone through her wan, pinched little face.

At once she became the pet of the whole party, and although she, in turn, liked them all, it was Professor Ditson who always held first place in her heart. If he were long away from her, she would call plaintively, *"Cariwa! Cariwa!"* the Arara word for white man. Sometimes she would sing, in her tiny voice, folk-songs which she had learned from her mother, all about the wonderful deeds and doings of armadillos, agoutis, and other South American animals.

Before long, however, in spite of careful nursing, she began to sink rapidly. Then came days when she sang no more, but lay too weak even to taste the fruits which the boys were always bringing in to her from the forest. At last one night Professor Ditson, who always slept close beside her, heard a little far-away voice whisper in his ear, "White man, dear, dear white man!" and felt the touch of her hand against his cheek. A moment later, under the light of the setting moon, he saw that Ala had gone where there is no more sickness nor pain and where little children are safe forever.

Later on, when the rest of the party roused themselves before sunrise for another day, they found the scientist sitting grim and impassive in the star-shine, still holding the tiny cold hand of the little Indian girl in his. When old Jud found that clenched tightly in Ala's other hand was the shell of a tree-snail, all white and pink and gold, which he had given her days before, the old man broke down and sobbed as he looked at the peaceful little figure.

Under the light of Achenar, Canopus, and the other eternal stars which flared through the blackness of the tropical night, they buried her deep at the foot of a vast paradise tree which had towered above the forest hundreds of years before the first white man ever came to South America and whose mighty girth will be standing when the last Indian of that continent has passed to his forgotten fathers. As Professor Ditson repeated over the little grave what part he could remember of the Service for the Dead, from the heart of the jungle sounded the deep, coughing roar of a jaguar as it wandered restless through the night.

The next day camp was broken and once more the party followed the trail through the forest. At first the gloom and grief of the little Indian girl's death hung over them all. Then, little by little, the healing of the forest began to be felt. The vast waiting trees, the bird-songs, the still beauty of the flowers all seemed to bring to them the joy and hope and faith which is the portion of wanderers among the solitudes and silences of earth.

The trail still ran, a dividing line between the steaming jungle on one side and the plateaus and foot-hills on the other. Behind the latter towered range after range of mighty mountains, among whose chill heights were hidden forgotten Inca cities and the lost treasure-lake of Eldorado. On the mountain side of the trail the trees were set farther apart and belonged to families from the temperate zone, while here and there were small parks covered with short grass, with bare, treeless slopes beyond.

It was in such a country, after several days to travel, that Pinto, Jud, and the two boys started on a hunt, while the others made camp. They had been out less than an hour when the sharp eyes of the old trapper spied two strange animals feeding in an open space hedged in by thickets. They had long, banded tails, which clanked and rattled as they moved. Moreover, they wore armored hides, set with square plates of bone and ringed around the middle with nine horny bands,

while big pricked-up ears, like those of the
rabbit, and long sheep eyes made them appear
to the old trapper as among the strangest animals he had ever met.

"Armadillos," whispered Pinto, delightedly, as he too caught sight of them. "Spread
out and we'll catch 'em both. Better 'n roast
pig to eat."

In a minute the four hunters had made a
wide circle around the unwary animals. It
was not until they were close to them that the
pair took alarm. Stopping their feeding,
they suddenly squatted with their fore legs off
the ground, much as a woodchuck might do.
Instead of curling up like porcupines and
trusting to their armor for protection, as Jud
had expected them to do, they suddenly
dropped on all fours and rushed and rattled
down the slope toward the old trapper, like
two small armored tanks, almost as fast as a
rabbit would run. Jud was as much surprised
as if he had seen a tortoise start to sprint.
Going like race-horses, they bore down upon
the old man.

"Hi! hi! stop! shoo!" bellowed Jud, waving both his arms over his head. "What 'll I do to stop 'em?"

"Trip 'em up," volunteered Will, from where he stood.

"Catch 'em by the tail!" yelled Joe. "Don't let 'em scare you."

In another minute they were upon him. Dodging his outstreched hands, their wedge-shaped heads plunged between his legs. Jud's feet flew up, and he sat down with a startling bump, while, rushing and clanking through the bushes, both of the armadillos disappeared in the depths of the thicket. The old man rose slowly and felt himself all over.

"I 'd just as soon try to stop a racing automobile with my two hands as to head off a scared armadillo," he observed indignantly. "They got no right to run that way. Their business is to curl up an' be caught."

"Never mind, Jud," said Will, comfortingly; "you had the right idea, but you tackled 'em a mite too high."

That day, as they rested after lunch, Will wandered up toward the mountains, as usual studying his beloved birds. Along the pampas-like stretches of the plateaus and up among the hills, he found the bird life very different from what it was in the jungle. It was Pinto who taught him the bassoon notes of the crested screamer, changing at times to the long roll of a drum, and pointed out to him "John o' the mud-puddles," the South American oven-bird, which, unlike the northern bird of the same name, builds a mud nest a foot or more in diameter, strengthened with hair and weighing several pounds. The birds mate for life, and have a quaint habit of singing duets while standing facing each other. Then there was another bird which Pinto called the "fire-wood gatherer," which built great nests of sticks in trees, dropping a wheelbarrow load of twigs under each nest. Of all the new birds, the boy liked the one called the "little cock" the best. These were ground-birds some nine inches long, with little tails that stuck straight upward, and bristling crests on their heads. Looking like small bantam roosters, they scurried around through the brush, following the travelers inquisitively and giving every now and then a loud, deep chirp. Whenever Will would chase one, it would scurry off, chirping with alarm, but always returned and followed him through the grass and brush.

As the days went by, Professor Ditson became more and more uneasy, and, when camp was pitched, overtaxed his unrestored strength by hunting through dark nooks in the jungle and peering and prying among tangles of fallen trees or the rare ledges of rock which showed now and then among the waves of green. At last he told the rest of the party the cause of his anxiety.

"In a few days more," he said, "we shall begin to climb the foot-hills of Peru. Under my contract with Mr. Donegan, we were to collect a bushmaster before we began the search for emeralds. So I would suggest that we make our camp here and scatter out through the jungle until one of us is fortunate enough to discover a specimen of this rare and beautiful serpent. Let me beg of you, however," he continued earnestly, "to use the utmost care in catching a bushmaster. They are easily injured."

Jud's face was a study. "I will," he promised. "I 'll bet there is n't any one on the continent of South America who will use more care than me."

The next day the first hunt began. Armed with long, forked sticks, the six adventurers poked their way painstakingly through the thickest parts of the jungle, but without any success so far as bushmasters were concerned, although Pinto aroused a fine specimen of a boa-constrictor, one of the smaller boas of South America, which flowed through the forest like a dark shimmering stream, while Jud scared up another hideous iguana, it being a disputed question as to which ran away the faster.

Toward the end of the afternoon Will found himself some distance from the others, following what seemed a little game trail, which zigzagged back and forth through the jungle. At one point it led between two great trees, and there Will caught sight of a blaze on either side of the path. As he stepped forward to examine the marks more carefully, a dreadful thing happened. The ground under his feet suddenly sank away without a sound, and the next moment he found himself at the bottom of a jug-shaped pit some fifteen feet deep, whose sides curved in so sharply that not even a monkey, much less a man, could climb out. The opening had been covered over with the stretched skins of animals, stitched together and cunningly hidden under turf and leaves.

Although shaken and half-stunned by his sudden fall, the soft earth floor of the trap saved him from any serious injury. Far above he could see the light streaming in through the irregular hole which his weight had made in the covering which masked the pit. All too late Will realized that the blazes on the sides of the game path had been warnings for human beings to avoid the pit-fall which they marked. The neck of the great earthen bottle was some five feet in width, but at the base it widened into a space fully double that distance across. As the boy's eyes became accustomed to the half-light below, he found that he could see the sides and the bottom of the pit more and more clearly, and, scrambling to his feet, he started to explore its full circumference.

At the first step came a sound which no man born of woman has to hear more than once in order to stand stone-still—a fierce, thick hiss. Stopping dead in his tracks, Will moved slowly back until he was pressing hard against the earthen wall behind him. Even as he stopped, from the half-darkness before him, with a dry clashing of scales, glided into the center of the pit, with sure, deadly swiftness, the pinkish-yellow and black-banded coils of a twelve-foot serpent. From its eyes, with their strange oval pupils, a dark streak stretched to the angles of the mouth from which a long, forked tongue played like a black flame. As the fierce head crested the triple row of many-colored coils, Will saw the curious hole between eye and nostril, the hall-mark of a deadly clan, and knew that before him was the king of all the pit-vipers—the dreaded bushmaster.

He stared into the lidless, fatal eyes of the

snake, as they shone evilly through the dusk until it seemed as if his heart would stop beating and icy drops stood on his forehead, for he knew from talks had with Professor Ditson that bushmasters possess a most uncertain temper, and he feared that this one might instantly attack him. Once he tried to move to a point farther along the circumference of the earthen circle. At the first stir of his cramped muscles, the great snake hissed again and quivered as if about to strike. Will settled despairingly back, resolved to move no more; yet ever his thoughts kept running forward to the long, dark hours which were to come, when he would be alone through the night with this terrible companion. Then if, overcome by sleep or cramp, he should move, he feared horribly to be stricken down in the dark by the coiled death that watched him.

Suddenly, as he set himself against making the least stir of a muscle, he heard from the jungle through the broken covering of the trap, the same far-reaching whisper of death which had sounded when he was hunting with

Pinto. A moment later, with staring eyes, he saw a black stream move sibilantly down the opposite wall of the pit, and realized that the blind black ants of the jungle were upon him —and that there was no escape.

Slowly the head of the moving column approached the bottom of the pit, and Will remembered in sick horror how the ants had torn away shred after shred of living flesh from the tortured body of the agouti. As the insatiable, inexorable mass rolled toward him, the bushmaster seemed either to hear or scent its approach. Instantly its tense coils relaxed, and it hurried around and around three sides of the pit, lashing upward against the perpendicular walls in a vain attempt to escape. In its paroxysm of terror, it came so close to the motionless boy that its rough, sharp scales rippled against his legs. Only when the van of the ant-army actually reached the floor of the pit and began to encircle its whole circumference did the great serpent seem to remember Will's presence. Then, as if entreating the help of a human being, it forced itself back of him, and, as the ants came nearer, even wound its way around Will's waist in an attempt to escape.

For a moment the fearful head towered level with the boy's face. Instinctively, Will's hand flashed out and caught the bush-master by the neck. It made no attempt to strike, nor even struggled under the boy's choking grip; only the coiled body vibrated as if trembling at the approach of the deadly horde. For a moment the advance of the ant-army seemed to stop, but it was only be-cause, in accordance with its tactics, the head of the column began to spread out until the base of the pit was a solid mass of moving ants and the black tide lapped at Will's very feet. Half-turning, and placing his ankles instead of his heels against the sides of the wall, the boy gained a few inches on the ris-ing pool of death that stretched out before him, while the straining body of the bush-master vibrated like a tuning-fork.

By this time, the opposite wall of the pit was covered and the whole circle of the base of the cone-shaped pit black and moving, except the little arc where Will stood. The ants were so close that he could see the monster heads of the leaders, and the pit was full of the whisper of their moving bodies flowing forward. Will shut his eyes and every muscle of his tense body quivered as if already feeling their ripping, shearing mandibles in his flesh.

Just as the front line of the fatal legion touched his shoes, something struck him on the head, and he opened his eyes to see a liana dangling in front of him, while the light at the entrance of the pit was blurred by old Jud's head and shoulders. With his free hand, Will reached forward and seized the long vine, to find it ending in a bowline-knot whose noose never gives.

"Slip it under your arms," called down the old trapper, hoarsely, "an' hang on! We'll pull you up."

It was the work of only a second to carry out the old man's instructions. Thrusting the loop over his head and under his arms, the boy gripped the tough vine with his left hand and tightened his cluch around the unresisting body of the great bushmaster.

"I won't leave you behind for those black devils," he murmured, as if the snake understood, and tugged at the liana rope as a signal that he was ready to start. In an instant he was hauled aloft, just as the ants swarmed over the space where he had stood. Fending himself off from the slanting walls with his feet, Will went up with a rush and through the opening at the top almost as fast as he had entered it. Close to the rope stood old Jud, with face chalky-white as he watched the army of ants pouring down into the pit, while Hen, Joe, and Pinto, and even Professor Ditson, hauled with all their might on the vine.

Jud had become uneasy at Will's long absence and had tracked him to the entrance of the trap just as the army-ants reached it. His shouts had brought the rest, and it was Hen Pine who, with his machete, had cut the supple liana and knotted the noose which had reached Will just in time. Directed by

Jud, his rescuers hauled on the vine so vigorously that the boy shot out of the pit and was dragged several yards along the ground before they knew that he was safe.

Jud hurried to help him up, but promptly did a most creditable performance in the standing-back broad-jump.

"Bring your machete here, quick!" he shouted to Hen; "a bushmaster's got the kid!"

"No," corrected Will, scrambling to his feet with some difficulty and waving off Hen with his unoccupied hand, "the kid's got a bushmaster."

Professor Amandus Ditson was delighted to his heart's core.

"That is the finest specimen of the *Lachesis mutus*," he remarked, as he unwound the rough coils from Will's waist, "that has ever been reported. Whatever happens now," he went on, relieving Will of his burden, "the trip is an unqualified success."

"The man's easily satisfied," murmured Jud, watching from a safe distance the professor grip the snake by the back of its neck and push it foot by foot into a long snake-bag which he always carried for possible specimens. When at last the bag, filled with snake, was tied tightly, it looked much like a long, knobby Christmas-stocking. The professor swung it carelessly over his shoulder like a blanket-roll.

"No snake ever bites through cloth," he remarked reassuringly. "Now for the Inca Emerald!"

CHAPTER X

SKY BRIDGE

AT the end of their next day's journey the Trail began to swing away from the jungle, and thereafter led ever upward, skirting the foot-hills of the mountain-ranges beyond which lay the lost cities of the Incas. Three days after Will's escape from the pit he found himself once more in terrible danger. During the siesta period at noon he had walked away from the rest of the party to see what new birds he might find. Not far from the camping-spot he came to a place where a colony of crested black-and-gold orioles had built long, hanging nests of moss and fiber among the branches of a low tree.

Curious to see whether their eggs looked like the scrawled and spotted ones of the Northern orioles, Will started to climb the tree.   Before he was half-way to the nests, a cloud of clamoring birds were flying around his head, and as he looked up he noticed for the first time, directly above him, a great gray wasps' nest.   Even as he looked, one of the circling birds brushed against it, and a cloud of enormous red wasps poured out. They paid no attention whatever to the birds, but flew down toward Will, who was already scrambling out of the tree at full speed.

Even as he reached the ground, two of the wasps settled on his bare arm, and instantly he felt as if he had been stabbed by red-hot daggers.   Never in his life had the boy known such agony.   Trembling with pain, he brushed the fierce insects off and rushed at top speed toward the camp.   In spite of the heat, a racking chill seized him as he ran. His teeth chattered together and waves of nausea seemed to run over his whole body, dimming his eyes and making his head swim. He just managed to reach the rest of the party when he staggered and fell.

"I 've been stung by some big red hornets,"

he murmured, and dropped back unconscious.

"It's the maribundi wasp," said Professor Ditson, looking very grave as he helped Hen undress the boy and sponge his tortured body with cold water. "Three of their stings have been known to kill a man."

By evening Will was delirious. All night long Hen and the scientist worked over him, and by the next day he was out of danger, although still in great pain and very weak. It was several days before he could walk, and then only with the greatest difficulty. At first every step was an agony; but Professor Ditson assured him that regular exercise was the best way to free his system from the effect of the maribundi venom.

Once again death which had dogged the adventurers' trail for so long peered out at them. They had finished the first stage of their day's walk, and Will was lying white and sick under a tree, trying to gain strength enough to go on. Ahead of them stretched a wide river, with a ford showing, down to which the Trail led. Suddenly from the depths of the near-by jungle came a horrid scream, followed by a chorus of baying notes something between the barking of a dog and the howl of a wolf. As the travelers sprang to their feet, a shower of blood-red arrows, with saw-edged points and barbs fashioned from flinty strips of palm-wood, dropped all around them. Again the wailing, terrible cry broke the silence.

"It's the jaguar-scream—the war-cry of the Miranhas," said Professor Ditson quietly. "They are on our trail with one of their packs of wild dogs."

Even as he spoke, from the forest far below them a band of Indians broke into the open. Ahead of them raced a pack of tawny brown dogs nearly as large as the timber-wolves of the North.

Hen unsheathed his great machete, while Jud fumbled with the holster of his automatic.

"No! no!" said Professor Ditson sharply. "We can stand them off better across the river. Hurry!"

Without a word, Hen picked up Will's limp body and raced ahead of the others around a bend in the trail which hid them all for a moment from the sight of their pursuers. At the river the scientist suddenly halted, after a long look at the rapids which ran deep and swift on each side of the ford.

"Don't splash as you go through," he said quietly. "I 'll come last."

One by one, the little party, headed by Hen with Will in his arms, waded carefully through the shallow water. As they went Jud thought that he caught glimpses in the river of the squat, fierce forms of the dreaded piranhas, but if they were there they paid no attention to the men, who crossed with the utmost care. Just as Professor Ditson, the last of the party to leave the bank, stepped into the stream, there sounded with startling distinctness the same wild chorus which had come from the jungle. Once or twice in a life-time a hunter in South American forests hears the fearsome screech which a jaguar gives when it is fighting for its life or its mate. It was this never-to-be-forgotten sound which the Miranhas had adopted for their war-cry.

Down the slope not three hundred yards away came the hunting pack. Right behind them, running nearly as fast as they, raced a band of some fifty Miranhas warriors. As the fugitives looked back it was not the nearness of the wild-beast pack nor the fierce band of Indian warriors rushing down upon them which struck the color from the faces of Will and Joe. It was the towering figure of a man with a black bar of joined eyebrows across his forehead and a scar on his cheek which twisted his face into a fixed, malignant grin.

"Scar Dawson!" muttered Will.

"Scar Dawson!" echoed Joe, despairingly.

As they spoke the outlaw seemed to recognize them too, for he waved aloft a Miranha bow which he carried, and shouted hoarsely. By the time they reached the other bank, Will lay half-fainting in Hen's arms.

"Fellows," he whispered, "I'm all in. Hide me in the bushes here, and you go on.

There's no sense in all of you sacrificing yourselves for me."

"We stay," murmured Joe, while Hen nodded his head and Pinto fitted one of his fatal little arrows into his blow-gun.

"Sure, we'll stay," chimed in Jud, unslinging his automatic, "an' there's seven Injuns who'll stay too unless I've forgotten how to shoot. But what in the world's the perfesser doin'?" he went on, peering out over the river.

Unheeding the tumult of howls and screeches behind him, or the rush of the fierce hounds and fiercer men toward him, the eminent scientist was picking his way carefully through the ford. At the middle of the river, where the water ran deepest, he rolled up his left sleeve, and with his hunting-knife unconcernedly made a shallow gash through the skin of his lean, muscular forearm. As the blood followed the blade he let it drip into the running water, moving forward at the same time with long, swift strides. Almost in a moment the river below the ford began to bubble and boil with the same rush of the fatal hordes which had so horrified Jud and Will at the Lake of the Man-eaters. As Professor Ditson sprang from the water to the edge of the farther bank, the water clear across the river seemed alive with piranhas. Unmoved, he turned to the rest of the party.

"That ford is locked," he said precisely. "For three hours it can not be crossed by man or beast."

Even as he spoke, the wild-dog pack splashed into the river. As they reached the deeper water and began to swim, the flash of hundreds of yellow-and-white fish showed ahead of them. In an instant the water bubbled like a caldron gleaming with myriads of razor-edged teeth. There was a chorus of dreadful howls as, one by one, the fierce dogs of the jungle sank below the surface, stripped skeletons almost before their bodies reached the bottom of the river. From the farther bank came a chorus of wailing cries as the warparty watched the fate of their man-hunting pack. Then, as if at some signal, the whole band threw themselves on their backs on the ground. Only the towering figure of the giant outlaw remained erect.

"What 's happened to those chaps?" queried Jud, much perplexed. "I 've been with Injuns nigh on to forty year, but I never see a war-party act that way."

As he spoke, Professor Ditson reached the summit of the slope where the rest of the party were standing, and saw the prostrate band on the other side of the river.

"Hurry out of here!" he said sharply, racing around a bend in the trail, followed by the others.

Their retreat was none too soon. Even as they started, each of the men of their far-away pursuers braced both his feet expertly against the inside horn of his bow, and fitting a five-foot arrow on the string, pulled with all the leverage of arms and legs combined, until each arrow was drawn nearly to its barbed point. There was a deep, vibrating twang that could be heard clearly across the river, and into the sky shot a flight of roving shafts. Up and up they went until they disappeared from sight, only to come whizzing down again from a seemingly empty sky, with such force and accuracy that they buried themselves deep into the ground just where the fugitives had been a minute before.

Jud, who had lingered behind the others, had a narrow escape from being struck by one of the long shafts.

"We 'd have all looked like porcupines if we 'd stayed there thirty seconds longer," he remarked to Joe, as he joined the rest of the party. "Them Miranhas are sure the dandy shots with a bow."

"Huh!" returned Joe jealously, "that nothing. My uncle out in Akotan, where I come from, he kill a man with an arrow half a mile away, and no use his feet either."

"That uncle of yours was some performer with a bow," returned Jud cautiously. "Half a mile is good shootin' even with a rifle."

"Some performer is right," chimed in Will weakly. "I learned long ago, when Joe and I were up by Wizard Pond, that that uncle of his held a world record in everything."

"Set me down, Hen," he went on. "I think I can do a mile or so on my own legs."

"From here on Pinto and I have been over this route," announced Professor Ditson. "Ten miles farther on is 'Sky Bridge.' If we can cross that and cut it behind us, we're safe."

Two by two, the members of the party took turns in helping Will along the Trail, which soon widened into a stone-paved road.

"This is one of the Inca highways," explained the scientist. "It leads from their first city clear to the edge of the jungle. Once," he went on, "the Incas ruled an empire of over a million square miles, equal to the whole United States east of the Mississippi River; but they never were able to conquer the jungle."

The road sloped up more and more steeply, and the going became increasingly difficult, but Professor Ditson hurried them on remorselessly.

"The Miranhas never give up a chase," he said, "and if they have succeeded in crossing

the river above or below the ford, they may
even now be hard on our heels."

Before long they were in a wilderness of
bare, stern peaks whose snow-covered summits towered high against the horizon. At
times the road zigzagged along narrow
shelves cut in the faces of precipices and
guarded here and there by low retaining-
walls built of cut stones laid without mortar,
but so perfectly that the blade of a knife could
not be thrust between them. The air became
colder, and the scientist told them that often
the temperature in these mountain-valleys
would vary as much as one hundred degrees
within twenty-four hours.

As they approached the crest of a great
ridge which towered above them, Jud began
to find great difficulty in breathing and complained of nausea and a feeling of suffo-
cation.

"It's the *soroche,* the mountain-sickness,"
explained Professor Ditson. "It will pass
soon."

"I'm the one that's goin' to pass—pass
out," panted Jud.

Soon he became so exhausted that, like Will, he had to be half-carried along the trail.

"You an' me are a fine pair to fight Injuns," he whispered to the boy, who smiled wanly in reply.

Beyond the ridge the road ran downward toward a vast gorge. From its dark depths rose and fell at intervals the hoarse, roaring bellow of a river rushing among the rocks a thousand feet below.

"It is Apurinac, the Great Speaker," said Pinto.

As the trail led downward again, Jud began to feel better, and before long he was able to walk without any help.

At length, far below them, looking like a white thread against the threatening blackness of the cañon, they saw swinging in the wind a rude suspension bridge of the kind which travelers had used in these mountains ever since the days of the Incas. When Pinto, who knew the bridge well, learned that Professor Ditson intended to cross it at once, he was much disturbed.

"No one, Master," he protested, "ever

crosses it except at dawn before the wind comes up; nor should more than one at a time pass over it."

"To-day," returned the scientist grimly, "you are going to see six men cross this bridge in the middle of the afternoon, wind or no wind; and what's more, they are all going to cross together." And he waved his hand toward the road along which they had come.

Against the white side of the mountain which the trail skirted showed a series of moving black dots, while down the wind, faint and far away, came the tiger-scream of the Miranhas. They had found a way across the river, and once more were hard on the heels of the treasure-hunters.

Along the Inca road the little party hurried at breakneck speed. At one place it ran between a vertical wall of rock and a dizzy precipice. Farther on it led down by rude stairs partly cut in the rock and partly built out of stones. At one point it made a sudden turn with a low parapet built around it in a semicircle to keep descending travelers from slipping off into the depths below from their

own momentum. Once beyond this last dan-
ger-point, the fugitives found themselves before Sky Bridge itself.

So deep was the cañon that from the river
a thousand feet below the bridge seemed on
a level with the clouds and to deserve well
its name. It was made of two thick cables,
woven out of braided withes, which stretched
nearly a hundred yards from bank to bank of
the gorge. Between and below these ran
several smaller cables, fastened to the upper
two, which served as guard-rails. Sections
of cane and bamboo laid transversely across
the three lower cables, and tied on by strips
of rawhide, formed the flooring, which swung
four or five feet below the upper cables.

From far below came the stern roar of the
Speaker, and at the bottom of the sunless gulf
gleamed the white foam of the river as it
raged against masses of rent and splintered
stone. Over the abyss the bridge waved
back and forth in the gusts which all day long
swept through the gorge. At times, when the
frail structure caught the full force of the
wind, it swung fully ten feet out beyond its

center, hung a second, and then dropped back with a jar that threatened to snap the cables or hurl into the abyss any human being who was crossing the bridge.

Not for all the treasure of the Incas would any one of the party have risked the crossing. The fear of death, however, is a great incentive to brave deeds.

"I 'll go first," said Professor Ditson suddenly, "and see if it is possible to get over. Unless we cross this bridge within the next fifteen minutes, we 're all dead men."

Without further speaking, the scientist stepped out upon the swaying bridge and gripped the twisted cables firmly fixed in buttresses of stone. At first he shuffled along with short, cautious steps. In front of him the footway of bamboo strips sloped away sharply clear down to the swaying center of the bridge. From far below, up through the mists which half hid the river, soared a bird the size of a pigeon. As it circled up through a thousand feet of space, it seemed to grow and grow until, by the time it reached the level of the bridge, rocking on mighty motion-

It showed itself as the great condor of the Andes, the
second largest bird that flies

less wings, it showed itself as the great condor of the Andes, the second largest bird that flies. From its grim, naked head its cold eyes gazed evilly upon the man clinging to the swaying bridge, and then turned toward the little group huddled against the side of the precipice, as if counting them as additions to its larder of death. As the great vulture swept by, blotting out a stretch of sky as it passed, the wind hissed and sang through the quills of its enormous wings, taut and stiff as steel. Rocking, swaying, perfectly balanced in the rush of air that howled down the cañon, the bird circled over the bridge, and then, without a flap of its vast wings, dipped down into the depths below until, dwindling as it went, it disappeared in the spray of the prisoned river. To the travelers, no other sight could so have plumbed the depths that lay beneath the bridge. For a moment the scientist, sick and giddy, clung to the swaying cables which seemed to stretch tenuous as cobwebs across the sheer blackness of the abyss.

"Come back, Master," called Pinto. "No man can cross that bridge!"

"No man here will live who does n't cross this bridge," returned the professor, as the wind brought again to their ears the war-cry of the Miranhas.

Bending double and clinging desperately to the ropes woven from tough maguey fiber, he edged his way down the swaying slope, while the others watched him as if fascinated. At times the full force of the wind as it was sucked through the long cañon swung the bridge out so far that he had to lie flat and cling for his very life's sake. When, at last, he reached the lowest part of the curve, instead of climbing up to the safety of the opposite shore, the scientist deliberately turned around and, taking advantage of every lull and pause in the sudden gusts which bore down upon him, began the long steep, slippery climb back to the point from which he had started.

"He 's riskin' his life twice to show us the way," said old Jud, suddenly. "Come on! I 'm more ashamed to stay than I 'm scared to cross."

Foot by foot, clinging desperately to the

sagging, straining cables, Professor Ditson
fought his way back. When at last he re-
gained the safety of the cliff-side, his face was
white and drawn, and he was dripping
with sweat, while his hands were bleeding
from the chafing of the ropes; but there was
a compelling gleam in his eyes, and his voice,
when he spoke, was as precise and level as
ever.

"I have proved that it is perfectly possible
to go over this bridge in safety, and I believe
that the cables are strong enough to hold the
weight of us all," he said. "I will go first;
Hen will go last. Don't look down. Hang
on. Watch the man ahead, keep on going,
and we 'll get over—just in time."

He stretched his gaunt arm toward the trail,
where now the Miranha band was in plain
sight not half a mile away!

Again he turned and started out over the
bridge, which swayed and swung above the
death that roared far below. Without a word,
but with teeth clinched grimly, Jud tottered
after him, his long gray beard blowing in the
wind. Next came Pinto, shaking with fright,

but with a habit of obedience to his master stronger than his own conviction that he was going to his doom. Joe followed; and between him and Hen, who brought up the rear, was Will. As the full force of the wind struck the swinging structure, now loaded with their united weight, the taut cables and ropes creaked and groaned ominously, while now and again some weakened fiber would snap with a sudden report like a pistol-shot.

Down and down the first terrible incline crept the little train of desperate men. There were times when the bridge would swing so far out that only by clinging and clawing desperately at the guard-rope could the travelers keep from being tipped into the depths below. When that happened, each would grip the one next to him and, with linked arms and legs, they would make a human chain which gave and swung and held like the bridge itself. At last they reached the low-swung center of the bridge, and caught the full force of the wind, which howled down the gorge like a wolf. For a long minute they lay flat on their faces as the bridge swung forth and back like a pendulum.

As the gust passed, they heard close at hand the tiger-screech of the Miranhas rushing at headlong speed down the trail as they saw their prey once again escaping. Up the far-ther slope, crouching low and gripping des-perately with twining hands and feet, the fug-itives pressed on foot by foot. At the worst places Will felt Hen's mighty arms holding him tight to the swinging ropes, while from ahead Joe risked his life time and again to stretch out a helping hand to his friend.

By inches, by feet, by yards, they wormed their way up, until Professor Ditson was able to get a firm foothold on the side of the cliff, where a narrow path had been cut in the living rock. Even as he struggled to his feet, the war-party dashed around the sharp curve that led to the entrance of the bridge.

With all their courage and relentless vin-dictiveness, the Miranha band yet hesitated to cross where the white men had gone. As Jud and Pinto joined Professor Ditson on the little platform of rock which towered above the cañon, they saw their pursuers actually turn their heads away from the deep that opened at their feet, after one glance along the narrow swaying bridge by which alone it could be crossed. Then, with a fierce yell, they dropped their bows and, whipping out long, narrow-bladed knives from their belts, fell like furies upon the tough woven cables anchored among the rocks. It was Jud who first realized that they were trying to cut the bridge.

"Hurry for your life!" he called down to Joe, who, holding on to Will with one hand, was slowly hauling himself up the last few feet of the steep ascent. Even as he spoke, the taut cables began to quiver and sing like violin-strings transmitting with fatal clearness every cut and slash and chop of the destroyers at the other end. Will was half-fainting with the strain of the crossing, which his weakened body was not fitted to endure long. Jud's shout seemed to pierce the mist of unconsciousness which was slowly closing over his head, and he struggled upward with all his might.

In another minute Joe was near enough to be reached by the party on the landing, and three pairs of sinewy arms gripped him and pulled him upward, clinging to Will as he rose. Below him, Hen, bracing both feet, heaved the boy upward with the full force of his mighty arms. Just as Will reached the refuge of the cliff, with an ominous snapping noise the bridge began to sag and drop. Hen gave a desperate spring and wound one arm around a little pinnacle of rock which stood as a hawser-post for one of the cables, while Pinto and Joe gripped his other arm in mid-air, and pulled him to safety just as the far end of the bridge swished through the air under the knife-strokes of the Indians!

As, doubled by its drop, the full weight of the structure fell upon the strained cables, they snapped like threads and cables, ropes and footway rushed down into the abyss with a hissing roar which died away in the dim depths a thousand feet below.

CHAPTER XI

THE LOST CITY

HARDLY had the rumble of the falling bridge passed when Jud slipped his arm about Will's shoulders and half-led half-dragged the fainting boy around the corner of a great rock.

"Those yellin' devils shoot too straight for us to take any chances," he remarked briefly.

The same idea had come to the rest of the party, and they followed hard on the old trapper's heels. Here Professor Ditson again took the lead.

"It 'll take them some time to get across that river, now the bridge is down, if they follow us," he observed with much satisfaction. "We ought to reach Machu Pichu to-day and Yuca Valley in two days more. There we 'll be safe."

"What 's Machu Pichu, Chief?" questioned

Jud, using this title of respect for the first time; for the professor's behavior at the bridge had made an abiding impression on the old man's mind. "It was the first city that the people of the Incas built," explained Professor Ditson.

"When the Inca clan first led their followers into these mountain valleys, they were attacked by the forest-dwellers and driven back into the mountains. There they built an impregnable city called Machu Pichu. From there they spread out until they ruled half the continent. Only the forests and the wild tribes that infested them they never conquered. At the height of the Inca Empire," went on the scientist, "Machu Pichu became a sacred city inhabited mostly by the priests. After the Spanish Conquest it was lost for centuries to white men until I discovered it a few years ago."

"Where do we go from Yuca?" questioned Jud again.

"Follow the map to Eldorado," returned the Professor, striding along the path like an ostrich.

Beyond the rock, and out of sight of the cañon, gaped the mouth of a tunnel fully three hundred yards in length. Narrow slits had been chiseled through the face of the precipice for light and air, and although cut out of the living rock with only tools of hardened bronze by the subjects or captives of forgotten Incas, it ran as straight and true as the tunnels of to-day drilled by modern machinery under the supervision of skilled engineers. Through the slits the adventurers caught glimpses of the towering peak down which they had come, but there was no sign of their pursuers. In a moment they had vanished from the naked rock-face against which they had swarmed.

Joe stared long through one of the window-slits, while below sounded the hoarse, sullen voice of the hidden river.

"I not like their going so soon," he confided at last to Jud. "Perhaps that Dawson have another secret way down the mountain, as he did at Wizard Pond."

"It's not likely," returned Professor Ditson, who had overheard him. "At any rate, the only thing to do is to press on as fast as possible."

"Why did n't my snake-skin make us safe from those people?" inquired Joe, as they hurried along.

"Because," explained the scientist, "the Miranhas are an outlaw tribe who have no religion and keep no faith. Nothing is sacred to them."

Beyond the tunnel a wide pavemented road led around the rear of the mountain and then up and up and in and out among a wilderness of peaks, plateaus, cliffs, and precipices.

In spite of the well-paved path along which in the old days the Incas had sent many an expedition down into the Amazon Valley, the progress of the party was slow. Will became rapidly weaker and for long stretches had to be helped, and even carried along the more difficult parts of the path.

Hour after hour went by. Once they stopped to eat and rest, but their tireless leader hurried them on.

"We 're not safe on this side of Machu Pichu," he said.

Will pulled himself to his feet.

"I'm the one who's keeping you all back," he said weakly. "From now on I walk on my own legs!" And, in spite of the others' protests, he did so, forcing his numbed nerve-centers to act by sheer strength of will. Toward the middle of the afternoon the path turned an elbow of rock, and in front of them towered a chaos of grim and lonely peaks, spiring above cañons and gorges which seemed to stretch down to the very bowels of the earth. In the background were range after range of snow-capped mountains, white as the clouds banked above them, while in front showed a nicked knife-edge of dark rock. The professor's face lightened as he looked.

"On that ridge," he said, stretching out his arm, "lies the Lost City!"

The path led downward until, although it was early afternoon, it became dim twilight in the depths of dark cañons, and then, twisting like a snake, came back to the heights, skirting the edges of appalling precipices in a series of spirals. As the way reached the sum-

mit of the ridge it became narrower and narrower, and at intervals above it stood stone
watch-towers on whose ramparts were arranged rows of great boulders with which the
sentinels of the Incas could have swept an in-
vading army down to destruction in a moment. The path ended at last in a flight of
steps cut out of the solid rock, with a wall on
each side, and so narrow that not more than
two could walk up them abreast. It was past
sunset when the little party reached the last
step and stood on the summit of the wind-
swept ridge. In the east the full moon was
rising above the mountains and flooded the
heights with light white as melting snow.

Before them stretched the city of Machu
Pichu, its shadows showing in the moonlight
like pools of spilled ink. Lost, lonely, deserted by men for half a thousand years, the
great city had been the birth-place of the
Incas, who ruled mightily an empire larger
than that which Babylon or Nineveh or
Egypt held in their prime. In its day it had
been one of the most impregnable cities of the
world. Flanked by sheer precipices, it was

reached only by two narrow paths enfiladed by watch-towers, eyries, and batteries of boulders. To-night the terraces were solitary and the strange houses of stone and vast rock-built temples empty and forsaken.

In the moonlight this gray birth-place of an empire lay before the travelers from another age, silent as sleep, and, as they passed through its deserted streets, the professor told them in a half-whisper thousand-year-old legends which he had heard from Indian guides. At the far side stood the great watch-tower Sacsahuaman, guarding the other path, which spiraled its way up the slope of a sheer precipice half a mile high.

"The Inca who built that," said the professor, "gave the tower its name. It means 'Friend of the Falcon,' for the Inca boasted that the hawks would feed full on the shattered bodies of any foe who tried to climb its guarded heights."

On the summit of a sacred hill he showed them a square post carved out of the top of a huge rock whose upper surface had been smoothed and squared so that the stone pillar made a sun-dial which gave the time to the whole city. Near by lay Sayacusca, the "Tired Stone," a vast monolith weighing a thousand tons, which was being dragged to the summit by twenty thousand men when it stuck. As the carriers struggled to move its vast bulk, it suddenly turned over and crushed three hundred of them. Convinced that they had offended some of the gods, the stone was left where it fell, and the skeletons of its victims are beneath it to this day.

High above the rest of the city was the sacred Sun Rock. From it the sun itself was believed to rise, nor might it be touched by the foot of bird, beast, or man. At the height of the Inca Empire it was plated all over with gold, which the Peruvians believed fell to the earth as the tears of the sun, and with emeralds and, except during the Festival of the Sun, covered with a golden-yellow veil. To-day its glory had departed, and the tired travelers saw before them only a frayed and weather-worn mass of red sandstone.

Seated on its summit, the scientist showed them the street where, during the Festival of the Sun, the Inca would ride along a pavement made of ingots of silver on a horse whose mane was strung with pearls and whose shoes were of gold. Beyond the Sun Rock was the Snake Temple, which had three windows and whose solid stone walls were pierced with narrow holes through which the sacred snakes entered to be fed by the priests.

"We might camp there," suggested Professor Ditson. "It would make a large, comfortable house."

"No, no," objected Jud shudderingly. "No snake temple for me."

They finally compromised on Sacsahuaman, whose thick walls were slit here and there by narrow peep-holes and whose only entrance was by a narrow staircase of rock cut out of the cliff and guarded, like most of the entrance staircases, by rows of heavy boulders arranged along the ledge. Inside were long benches of solid stone, and, best of all, at the base of a white rock in the center of the tower trickled an ice-cold spring whose water ran through a little trough in the rock as it had run for a thousand years. Professor Ditson told them that in the old days it had always been kept guarded and munitioned as a fortress where the Incas could make a last stand if by any chance the rest of the city should ever fall into the hands of their enemies.

That night they kindled a fire within the tower, and ate their supper high above the sacred city on the battlements where the guards of the Incas had feasted a thousand years before Columbus discovered the New World. Afterward they slept, taking turns in guarding the two entrances to the city from the same watch-towers where other sentries had watched in the days of the beginning of the Inca Empire.

The next morning Will could not move. The stress and strain and exertion of the day before had left him too weak to throw off the numbing effect of the virus. Professor Ditson shook his head as he looked him over carefully.

"There is only one thing to do," he said at last. "We must send on ahead and get a horse or a burro for him. He has walked too much as it is. Any more such strain might leave him paralyzed for life. Hen," he went on, "you know the trail to Yuca. Take Joe and start at once. You ought to run across a band of vaqueros herding cattle long before you get to the valley. Bring the whole troop back with you. I'll pay them, well, and they can convoy us in case the Miranhas are still after us."

A few minutes later Hen and Joe were on their way. Leaning over the parapet of Sacsahuaman, the rest of the party watched them wind their way slowly down the precipice until they disappeared along the trail that stretched away through the depths of the cañon. All the rest of that day Jud and Pinto and the professor took turns in standing guard over the two entrances to the city, and in rubbing Will's legs and giving him alternate baths of hot and cold water, the recognized treatment for stings of the maribundi wasp.

That night it was Jud's turn to guard the staircase up which the party had come. Once, just before daybreak, he thought he heard far below him the rattle and clink of rolling stones. He strained his eyes through the dark, but could see nothing, nor did he hear any further sounds. In order, however, to discourage any night prowlers, the old trapper dropped one of the round boulders that had been placed in the watch-tower for just such a purpose, and it went rolling and crashing down the path.

Daylight showed the trail stretching away below him apparently empty and untrodden since they had used it when entering the city. Tired of waiting for Professor Ditson, Jud hurried up the steep slope to the fortress, meeting the scientist on the way to relieve him. The old trapper was just congratulating Will on being well enough to stand on his feet when a shout for help brought all three with a rush to the entrance of the tower. Up the steep slope they saw Professor Ditson running like a race-horse, while behind him showed the giant figure of Dawson, followed closely by half a hundred Miranhas. In another minute Professor Ditson was among them.

"They must have hidden during the night around a bend in the path and rushed up when we changed guards," he panted. "They were swarming into the tower just as I got there."

All further talk was stopped by the same dreadful tumult of war-cries that the travelers had learned to know so well.

"Steady, boys," said Jud, instantly taking command, as a veteran of many Indian fights. "Four against fifty is big odds, but we 've got a strong position. Will, you sit by the staircase an' if any one starts to come up, roll one of them fifty-pound boulders down on him, with my compliments. I 'll stay back here where I can watch the whole wall an' pick off any one that tries to climb up. Professor, you an' Pinto keep back of me, with your ax an' knife handy in case any of them get past me. Now," he went on, as the three took their stations, "how about some breakfast?"

After the first fierce chorus of yells there was a sudden silence. Led by Dawson, the Indians were far too crafty to attempt a direct charge up through the narrow gateway. The roofless walls, no longer raftered by heavy timbers, as in the Inca's day, were the weak spot in the defense of the besieged. If enough of the Miranhas succeeded in scaling them in

spite of Jud's markmanship, the defenders of
the fort could be overpowered by sheer weight
of numbers. While the little party of the besieged were eating breakfast at their several
stations, they could hear the sound of heavy
objects being dragged across the paved street
without, and the clink and jar of stone against
the wall. Always, however, the besiegers
kept themselves carefully out of the range of
vision from the tower's narrow loop-holes.
At noon Jud insisted that Pinto cook and
serve dinner as usual.

"Eat hearty, boys," the old Indian-fighter
said. "You may never have another chance.
I dope it out they're pilin' rocks against the
walls an' when they've got 'em high enough
they'll rush us."

It was the middle of the afternoon before
Jud's prophecy was fulfilled. For some time
there had been no sign nor sound from the
besiegers. Then suddenly, from six different and widely separated points in the semicircle of stone, hideous heads suddenly showed
over the edge of the wall, and, with the tiger-
scream of their tribe, five picked Miranha

warriors started to scramble over and leap down upon the little party below, while at the end of the curved line showed the scarred, twisted face and implacable eyes of the outlaw from the North.

It was then that the wiry little gray-bearded trapper showed the skill and coolness that had made his name famous throughout a score of tribal wars which had flickered and flared through the Far Northwest during his trapping days. Standing lithe and loose, he swung his automatic from his hip in a half-circle and fired three shots so quickly that the echo of one blended with the beginning of the next. Hard upon the last report came the pop of Pinto's deadly blow-gun. Three of the besiegers toppled over dead or wounded, and with a dreadful shout Scar Dawson clawed frantically at his shoulder where a keen thorn of death from Pinto's tube had lodged. The other two Indians scrambled down in terror, and there came a chorus of appalling screams, wails, and yells from the other side of the thick wall.

"I could have got 'em all," remarked Jud

Hideous heads suddenly showed over the edge of the wall

cheerfully, polishing his smoking automatic on his sleeve, "but I've only got four cartridges left an' we're likely to need 'em later. Will," he went on, "you just step over to the watch-tower there an' see if there're any signs of Hen an' Joe. A few South American cowboys would come in mighty handy just about now."

"If they don't come before night," stated Professor Ditson calmly, "we're gone. The Miranhas are certain to rush us as soon as it gets dark."

Even as he spoke, there came from outside a wail, swelling to a shriek like the unearthly scream of a wounded horse, yet with a note of triumph and anticipation running through it. Pinto started and shivered, while Professor Ditson's face showed grim and set.

"You'll have to get us first," he muttered.

"What do they mean by that little song?" inquired Jud coolly.

"It's the hag-cry that the women raise before they torture the prisoners," returned the other. "They think they're sure of us as soon as the sun goes down."

Will returned just in time to catch the last words.

"There's no one in sight," he said. "Could n't we slip off ourselves down the cliff?" he went on.

"Not a chance," explained the scientist. "They'd roll boulders down on us."

"Is there any way of holding them off after dark?" went on Will, after a little pause —and had his answer in the pitying silence of the two older men.

For a moment he turned very white. Then he set his teeth and threw back his shoulders.

"I'm only a kid," he said, "but I've been in tight places before. You need n't be afraid to talk plain."

"If they get over when it's too dark to shoot straight," said Jud at last, "we're all in."

Will looked at him unflinchingly.

"Watch the stairs," he said suddenly. "I've an idea." And the boy hurried back to the little parapet that overhung the trail that ran a thousand feet below.

Beyond and above him, the rim of the setting sun was coming nearer and nearer to the snow-capped mountains that cut the sky-line of the west. Already their white crests were gleaming crimson in the dimming light. As he went, Will fumbled in his belt and pulled out a tiny round pocket-mirror, which, with a tooth-brush, a comb, and a few other light articles, he had carried all through the trip in a rubber pocket fastened to his belt.

During these happenings, miles away, concealed by the intervening range, Hen and Joe were riding at the head of a troop of hard-bitten, hard-faced vaqueros, the cow-boys of the South, whom they had met at the end of their first day's journey. Armed with Mauser rifles, and with revolvers and knives in their belts, these riders of the pampas backed their wiry little South American horses with the same ease which their brethren of the Northern prairies showed.

The leader of the troop had turned out to be an old friend of Professor Ditson, who had been with him on an expedition years before. He readily agreed to journey with Joe and Hen over the mountains to the Lost

City. The men had been rounding up half a dozen hardy, tiny burros, those diminutive donkeys which can carry their own weight of freight all day long up and down steep mountain trails. It was decided to take these along for the use of the travelers. With the obstinacy of their breed, however, there was never a time throughout the day when one or more and sometimes all of the burros were not balking at this long trip away from the ranch where food and rest were awaiting them. Accordingly, it was late in the afternoon when the party reached the range behind which was hidden Machu Pichu.

Suddenly Joe, who with Hen, mounted on spare horses, was piloting the little troop, caught sight of a flicker of light across the crest of the highest peak of the range ahead of them. At first he thought that it came from the rays of the setting sun reflected from a bit of polished quartz. Suddenly he noticed, with a sudden plunge of his heart, that the light was flickering in spaced, irregular intervals. With Will and several of the other boys of his patrol, Joe had won a merit badge for signaling in his Boy Scout troop, and his tenacious Indian mind had learned forever the Morse code. As he watched now he saw the sun-rays flash the fatal S O S. Again and again came the same flashes, carrying the same silent appeal, which he knew could come from none other than Will behind the range, heliographing with the last of the sun to the chum who had stood back of him in many a desperate pinch.

As Joe glanced at the setting sun he realized how short a time was left in which to save his friends. With an inarticulate cry, he turned to Hen, who was jogging lazily beside him, and in a few quick words told him what he had read in the sky. With a shout Hen gave the alarm to the troop behind in the rolling Spanish of the pampas, and in an instant, hobbling the burros, every man was spurring his horse desperately up the steep trail. With the very last rays of the disappearing sun the message changed, and the Indian boy sobbed in his throat as he read the words.

"Good-by, dear old Joe," flickered in the sky.

As the golden rim of the sun rolled beneath the horizon, Will strained his eyes desperately, hoping against hope to see a rescue-party appear against the trail which showed like a white thread against the mountain-side. Suddenly, in the dimming light, he saw a few black dots moving against the crest of the opposite mountain. They increased in number, and, once over the ridge, grew larger and larger until Will could plainly make out a far-away troop of riders and glimpse the rush of straining horses and the stress and hurry of grim-faced men. With a shout he leaned far out over the parapet until in the distance the drumming beat of galloping hoofs sounded loud and louder.

Ten minutes later a long line of men with rifles in their hands were hurrying up the steep path that led to Sacsahuaman.

The besieged were not the only ones who knew of their coming. Outside of the walls of the fort, the Miranha band had understood Will's shout when he first saw the distant horsemen. They too had heard the hoof-beats, which sounded louder and nearer every minute, and, although the path up the precipice could be seen only from the fort, yet from without the besiegers could hear the clink of steel against the rocks and the murmur of the voices of the climbing men. Just before the rescue-party reached the fort, Jud's quick ear caught the sound of muttered commands, the quick patter of feet, and through a loophole he saw a black band hurrying toward the other entrance to the city, carrying with them the bodies of their dead and wounded comrades.

Even as he looked there was a shout, and into the little fortress burst the rescue-party, headed by Hen, and Joe. In another minute they swarmed through the streets of the city; but the enemy was gone. At the foot of the other path the last of them were even then slipping into the darkening valley.

Of all the band, alive or dead, one only had been left behind. Just outside the thick wall of the fort lay a huge motionless form. As Jud and Professor Ditson approached it they recognized Scar Dawson, deserted by the men whom he had so recently led. As they came close they saw that he lay helpless. Only his staring eyes were fixed upon them with an expression of awful appeal; yet there seemed to be no wound any where on his great body. As they bent over him, Pinto pointed silently to a tiny red spot showing at the front of the outlaw's right shoulder—the mark made by one of the Indian's fatal little arrows. Jud stared sternly down at the helpless man.

"You 've only got what was comin' to you," he said. "You 'd have tortured every one of us to death if you could," he went on but there was an uncertain note in his voice. "He 's a bad actor if ever there was one," he blustered, turning to the others. "Still, though, I 'd hate to see any man die without tryin' to help him," he finished weakly.

"He deserves death if any man ever did," said Professor Ditson grimly; "yet it does not seem right to let a man die without help."

"Yes," chimed in Will, looking down at the dying man pityingly; "do save him if you can."

The professor hesitated.

"Well," he said at last, "I can and I

will; but I am not at all sure that I ought."

Beckoning to one of the vaqueros, he took from his pouch a handful of the brown salt that is part of the equipment of every South American cattle-man. Reaching down, he forced open the stiffening jaws of the outlaw and pressed between them a mass of salt until Dawson's mouth was completely filled with it.

"Swallow that as fast as you can," he commanded.

Even as he spoke, the muscles of the man's great body relaxed as little by little the antidote for the urari poison began to work. Fifteen minutes later, tottering and white, but out of danger, the outlaw stood before them.

"I have saved your life," said Professor Ditson, "and I hope that you will make some better use of it than you have done. Your friends went down that way," he continued precisely, pointing to the path along which the Indians had retreated. "I would suggest that you follow them."

The outlaw stared scowlingly for a moment at the ring of armed men who stood around him. Then he turned to Professor Ditson.

"For saving my life I'll give you a tip which may save yours," he said thickly. "Don't treasure-hunt in Eldorado—*it's guarded!*" Without another word he disappeared down the steep trail.

"I hope I haven't made a mistake," murmured Professor Ditson to himself, as he watched Scar Dawson disappear in the distance.

CHAPTER XII

ELDORADO

A DAY and a night on burro-back brought the treasure-seekers through the mountains to Yuca, the loveliest valley in the world, where nine thousand feet above the sea it is always spring. There, half a thousand years ago, the Incas built their country houses, as of old the kings of Israel built in the mountain-valley of Jezreel, and among the ruins of stone buildings, beautiful as Ahab's house of ivory, several hundred whites and half-breed Indians had made their homes. In Yuca Professor Ditson found many old friends and acquaintances, and the party rested there for a week and, thanks to Jim Donegan's generous letter of credit, which had survived the shipwreck, thoroughly equipped themselves for the last lap of the dash to Eldorado.

One morning, before the dawn of what felt

like a mid-May day, the expedition headed back along the trail, mounted on mules the best and surest-footed animals for mountain work. In order to prevent any unwelcome followers, the professor allowed it to be supposed that they were going back for a further exploration of the sacred city of Machu Pichu. When at last they were clear of the valley, with no one in sight, he called a halt, and carefully consulted his map at a point where the trail led in and out among slopes and hillocks of wind-driven sand.

"Here is where we turn off," he said finally.

Jud suddenly produced two large, supple ox-hides which he had carried rolled up back of his saddle.

"So long as we're goin' treasure-huntin'," he remarked "an' Scar Dawson is still above ground, I calculate to tangle our trail before we start."

Under his direction, the whole party rode on for a mile farther, and then doubled back and turned off at right angles from the trail, Jud spreading rawhides for each mule to step on. Their progress was slow, but at the end

of half a mile they were out of sight of the
original trail and had left no tracks behind
except hollows in the sand, which the wind
through the day would cover and level.

For the next three days Professor Ditson
guided them by the map among a tangle of
wild mountains and through cañons so deep
that they were dark at midday. At night
their camp-fire showed at times like a beacon
on the top of unvisited peaks, and again like
a lantern in the depths of a well, as they
camped at the bottom of some gorge. Here
and there they came upon traces of an old trail
half-effaced by the centuries which had passed
since it had been used in the far-away days
when the Incas and their followers would
journey once a year to the sacred lake with
their annual offerings. Even although Professor Ditson had been to Eldorado before,
yet he found it necessary continually to refer
to the map, so concealed and winding was the
way.

On the third day they reached a wide pla-
teau which ranged just above the tropical
jungles of the eastern lowlands. At first they

crossed bare, burned slopes of rock, with here and there patches of scanty vegetation; but as they came to the lower levels they found themselves in a forest of vast cacti which seemed to stretch away for an immeasurable distance. Some of the larger specimens towered like immense candelabras sixty and seventy feet high, and there were clumps of prickly-pears as big as barrels and covered with long, dark-red fruit which tasted like pomegranates. Underfoot were trailing varieties which hugged the earth and through which the mules had to pick their way warily because of the fierce spines with which they were covered. Some of the club-cacti were covered with downy, round, red fruit fully two inches in diameter, luscious, sweet and tasting much like huge strawberries. Jud, who firmly believed that eating was one of the most important duties and pleasures of life, nearly foundered before they reached the pampas beyond the thorny forest. There they had another adventure in South American foods. As they were crossing a stretch of level plain, suddenly a grotesque long-legged bird started up from the tangled grass and, with long bare neck stretched out horizontally and outspread wings, charged the little troop, hissing like a goose as he came.

"Don't shoot!" called out Professor Ditson to the startled Jud, who was the nearest one to the charging bird. "It's only a rhea, the South American ostrich. He'll run in a minute."

Sure enough, the old cock rhea, finding that he could not frighten away the intruders by his tactics, suddenly turned and shot away across the level plain, his powerful legs working like piston-rods and carrying him toward the horizon at a rate of speed that few horses could have equaled. In the deep grass they found the nest, a wide circular depression containing thirty great cream-colored eggs, the contents of each one being equal to about a dozen hen's eggs. The Professor explained that the female rheas of each flock take turns laying eggs in the nest, which, as a fair division of labor, the cock bird broods and guards. After incubation starts the shell

turns a pale ashy gray. The party levied on
the rhea's treasure-horde to the extent of a
dozen glossy, thick-shelled eggs, and for two
days thereafter they had them boiled, fried,
roasted, and made into omlets, until Jud declared that he would be ashamed ever to look
a rhea in the face again.

At last, about noon of the fifth day after
leaving Yuca, the trail seemed to end in a
great wall of rock high up among the mountains. When they reached the face of this
cliff it appeared again, zigzagging up a great
precipice, and so narrow that the party had to
ride in single file. On one side of the path
the mountain dropped off into a chasm so
deep that the great trees which grew along its
floor seemed as small as ferns. Finally the
trail ended in a long, dark tunnel, larger and
higher than the one through which they had
passed on the way to Yuca. For nearly a
hundred feet they rode through its echoing
depths, and came out on the shore of an inky
little lake not a quarter of a mile across, and so
hidden in the very heart of the mountain that
it was a mystery how any one had ever dis-

covered it. Although it sloped off sharply
from its bare white beach, Professor Ditson
told them that it was only about twenty feet
deep in the center. A cloud of steam drifting lazily from the opposite shore betokened
the presence of a boiling spring, and the
water, in spite of the latitude, was as warm as
the sun-heated surface of the Amazon itself.

Leading the way, Professor Ditson showed
them, hidden around a bend, a raft which he
and his party had built on their earlier visit,
from logs hauled up from the lower slopes
with infinite pains. Apparently no one had
visited the lost lake since he had been there,
and a few minutes later the whole party were
paddling their way to the center of Eldorado, where lay hidden the untold wealth of
centuries of offerings.

"If I could have dived myself, or if any
of the Indians who were with me could have
done so," remarked the professor regretfully,
"we need not have wasted a year's time."

"Well," returned Jud, already much excited over the prospect of hidden treasure, "I
used to do over forty feet in my twenties, when

I was pearl-divin', an' now, though I 'm gettin' toward fifty, I certainly ought to be able
to get down twenty feet."

"Fifty!" exclaimed Will.

"Fifty!" echoed Joe.

"Fifty!" chimed in Professor Ditson.

"That 's what I said," returned Jud, looking defiantly at his grinning friends, "fifty or
thereabouts. I 'll show you," he went on
grimly, stripping off his clothes as they
reached the very center of the little lake, and
poising his lean, wiry body on the edge of the
raft. Suddenly he turned to Professor Ditson. "There ain't nothin' hostile livin' here
in this lake, is there?" he questioned.

"I don't think so," returned the professor,
reassuringly. "Piranhas are never found at
this height, and we saw no traces of any
other dangerous fish or reptiles when we were
here last year."

"Here goes then, for a fortune!" exclaimed
Jud, throwing his hands over his head and
leaping high into the air with a beautiful
jack-knife dive. His slim body shot down
out of sight in the dim, tepid water.

The seconds went by, with no sign of him, until he had been under fully three minutes. Just as they all began to be alarmed for his safety, his gray head suddenly shot two feet out of the water near where he had gone down. Puffing like a porpoise, with a few quick strokes he reached the edge of the raft and tossed on its surface something which clinked as it struck the logs.

There, gleaming in the sunlight, was a bird of solid gold, which looked like a crow, with outspread wings, and which was set thickly with rough emeralds as large as an ordinary marble.

With a cheer, Joe and Will gripped Jud's shoulders and pulled him over the side of the raft, where he lay panting in the sunlight, while the treasure was passed from hand to hand.

It was nearly a foot long, and so heavy that it must have handicapped the old man considerably in his dash for the surface.

"Pretty good for a start," puffed Jud happily, as he too examined the gleaming bird. "Unless I miss my guess," he went on earnestly, "the great emerald that old Jim has got his heart set on is down there, too.   The bottom is pretty well silted over, but I scrabbled through the mud with my hands, an' when I struck this I figured out that I had just enough breath left to reach the top; but just as I was leavin', my fingers touched somethin' oval an' big as a hen's egg.   It was pretty deep in the mud, and I didn't dare wait another second, but I'm sure I can bring it up next time."

For half an hour Jud rested while Professor Ditson told them treasure-stories which he had heard in his wanderings among the Indian tribes or remembered from his studies of Spanish archives.   He told them the story of the galleon *Santa Maria,* which was sunk off the Fortune Islands, loaded down with a great altar of solid gold incrusted with precious stones; and of the buccaneer Sir Henry Morgan, who sacked Panama and burned and sank in the harbor what he thought were empty vessels, but which held millions of dollars in gold and jewels in double bulkheads and false bottoms, and which lie to this day in the mud of Panama harbor.   Then, there was the

story of the two great treasure-chests which
Drake of Devon captured from the great galleon *Cacafuego*. As they were being trans-
shipped into Drake's vessel, the *Golden Hind,*
both of the chests broke loose and sank off
Caño Island on the coast of Costa Rica. Still
at the bottom of that tiny harbor, thousands
of pounds of gold bars and nuggets and a
treasure of pearls and emeralds and diamonds
lie waiting for some diver to recover them.
Then Professor Ditson launched into the story
of Pizarro's pilot, who, when the temple of
Pachacainac, twenty miles from Lima, was
looted, asked as his share of the spoils only the
nails that fastened the silver plates which
lined the walls of the temple. Pizarro
granted him what he thought was a trifling re-
quest, and the pilot received for his share
over two thousand pounds of solid silver.

"That's enough," said Jud, starting to his
feet. "Here goes for the biggest treasure of
all."

Down and down through the dim water he
dived straight and true. Hardly had he disappeared from sight before great air-bubbles

came up and broke on the surface, and a few seconds later wavering up from the depths came what seemed to be his lifeless body with staring, horrified eyes and open mouth.

As his white face showed above the surface, Will and Joe leaped in together, and in an instant had him out and on the raft again. In another minute the two boys were making good use of their knowledge of first aid, which they had learned as Boy Scouts. Working as they had never worked for merit badges, they laid Jud on the raft face down, with his arms above his head and his face turned a little to one side. Then, while Joe pulled his tongue out, Will, kneeling astride his body, pressed his open hands into the spaces on either side of his ribs. Then, alternately pressing and relaxing his weight as the water ran out of Jud's mouth and nose, Will began the artificial breathing at the rate of fifteen times a minute, while Joe rubbed with all his might the old trapper's legs and body toward the heart. At the end of a couple of minutes of this strenuous treatment Jud gave a gasp and at last opened his eyes. Half an hour later he was able to tell what had happened.

"I did n't get more than half-way down," he said weakly, "when a great greenish-yellow eel, five feet long an' big as my arm, came gliding toward me. I tried to pass it but in a second I felt its cold, clammy body pressin' against mine. Then came a flash, an' somethin' broke in my head, an' the next thing I knew I was up here with you chaps workin' over me."

Professor Ditson brought his hands together with a loud clap.

"That is what Dawson meant by saying the lake was guarded," he said. "What attacked Jud here was a gymnotus."

"A Jim-what?" queried Jud.

"An electric eel," explained the Professor. "The old priests must have brought them up from the lowlands, and they have thrived here in this warm water ever since. It carries an electric battery in the back of its head, and a big one can give a shock which will stun a strong man. Wait a moment," he went on, "and I 'll show you every electric eel within a radius of fifty yards."

As he spoke he fumbled in his knapsack and pulled out a cylinder two feet long, wrapped in waxed paper, with a curious little clock-work attachment at one end.

"I brought along two or three sticks of dynamite equipped with detonators," explained the professor. "They are really small depth-bombs. I thought," he went on, "that if the mud were too deep at the bottom of the lake, a stick or so of dynamite exploded there might stir things up. I 'll set this one to go off half-way down, and the shock will stun every living thing in the water for a couple of hundred feet around."

Winding and setting the automatic mechanism so as to explode the bomb at a ten foot depth, the scientist carefully threw one into the water some distance from the raft. Two seconds later there was a dull, heavy *plop*, and the water shouldered itself up in a great wave which nearly swamped the raft. As it went down, scores of fish of different kinds floated stunned on the surface. Among them were a dozen great green-gold electric eels. As they floated by, Hen slashed each one in two with his machete.

As he finished the last one, Will began to strip off his clothes.

"I can dive twenty feet," he said, "and I'm going to have the next chance at the Inca Emerald."

"No," objected Professor Ditson, "Let Hen try it. He's a great swimmer."

Jud also protested weakly that he wanted to go down again; but Will cut short all further argument by diving deep into the center of the still heaving circle of widening ripples in front of the raft. Even as he did so, Hen, who had stood up to take his place, gave a cry of warning; but it was too late to reach the boy's ears, already deep under the water. Just beyond the circle of the ripples drifted what seemed to be the end of a floating snag; yet the quick eyes of the negro had caught the glint of a pair of green, catlike eyes showing below the tip of a pointed snout which looked like a bit of driftwood.

"It's a big 'gator," he murmured to Professor Ditson, who stood beside him.

The latter took one look at the great pointed head and olive-colored body, now showing plainly in the water.

"It's worse than that," he whispered, as if afraid of attracting the saurian's attention. "It's an American crocodile. The explosion and the sight of the dead fish have brought it over from the farther shore."

Without paying any attention to the raft or the men, the great crocodile suddenly sank through the water, so close to them that they could see its triangular head, with the large tooth showing on each side of its closed lower jaw, which is one of the features that distinguishes a crocodile from an alligator. Even as they watched, wavering up through the smoky water came the white figure of the boy from the depths below, swimming strongly toward the surface, his right hand clasped tightly around some large object. Even as they glimpsed the ascending body, a gasp of horror went up from the little group on the raft. Before their very eyes, with a scythe-like flirt of its long, flattened tail, the great reptile shot its fifteen-foot body down toward the swimming boy.

Not until fairly overshadowed by the rushing bulk of the crocodile did Will realize his danger. Then he tried frantically to swerve out of the line of the rush of this terrible guardian of the treasure-horde. It was too late. Even as he swung away, the cruel jaws of the great saurian opened with a flash of curved keen teeth and closed with a death-grip on Will's bare thigh.

With a shout and a splash, the black form of the giant negro shot down into the water. Hen had learned to love the happy-hearted, unselfish boy, and, desperate at the sight of his danger, had gone to his rescue. No man nor any ten men can pull apart the closed jaws of a man-eating crocodile. The plated mail in which he is armored from head to tail can not be pierced by a knife-thrust and will even turn aside a bullet from any except the highest powered rifles. Yet all the crocodilians— alligators, crocodiles, gavials, or caymans— have one vulnerable spot, and Hen, who had hunted alligators in Florida bayous, knew what this was.

Swimming as the onlookers had never seen man swim before, the great negro shot toward the crocodile, which was hampered by the struggling boy, locked his strong legs around the reptile's scaly body, and sank both of his powerful thumbs deep into the sockets of the crocodile's eyes. The great saurian writhed horribly as he felt the rending pain. Inexorably the thumbs of his assailant gouged out the the soft tissues of the eye-sockets until the crocodile reluctantly loosed his grip and sought refuge from the unbearable pain by a rush into the deeps beyond the raft. As the great jaws opened, Hen unwound his legs from the armored body, and, catching Will in his mighty arms, shot up to the surface with him.

In another moment the boy, slashed and torn, but conscious, was stretched on the raft beside Jud, while Joe and the professor bound up the gashes in his thigh, which, although bleeding profusely, were not deep enough to be dangerous. As the last knot of the hasty bandages was tied, Will smiled weakly and opened his right hand. There, in the outstretched palm, gleamed and coruscated the green glory of a great oval emerald, cut and polished by some skilful lapidarist perhaps a thousand years ago. Lost for centuries, the gem which had been worshiped by a great nation had once again come to the earth from which it had disappeared.

Three weeks later, Professor Amandus Ditson lay sleeping in a luxurious bedroom on the ground floor of the rambling house of a Spanish friend whom he was visiting in the beautiful, historic, blood-stained city of Lima. In other rooms of the same house slept Will and Jud and Joe. Two days later the steamer would sail which was to take them all back north. Pinto was already on his way back to his wife and children at Para, and Hen was visiting friends of his own in the city and intended to join the party on the steamer.

The silence of the night was broken abruptly by a grating, creaking noise, and into the room of the sleeping scientist through the veranda window stepped a great masked fig-

ure.   As the electric lights were switched on,
Professor Ditson awoke to find himself looking into the barrel of an automatic revolver.

"Give me the treasure from Eldorado,"
croaked a voice from behind the mask, "if you
want to keep on livin'."

The scientist stared steadily at the speaker
for a moment before he spoke.

"If you will take off your mask, Dawson,"
he said finally, "I am sure you will find it
more comfortable.   I was positive," he went
on, as the other obeyed and showed the scarred,
scowling face of the outlaw, "that I made a
mistake in sparing your life."

"I 'll spare yours, too," retorted Dawson,
"unless you make me kill you.   I 'm goin' to
take the treasure an' light out.   It would be
much safer for me to kill you, but I won't unless I have to—just to show you how grateful
I am."

"I appreciate your consideration," returned
the scientist, quietly; "but you 're too late.
The treasure is not here."

"I know better," growled Dawson.   "I 've
had you shadowed ever since you got here.

It's locked in that leather bag, which never leaves your sight day or night, an' I'm goin' to take it right now."

Suiting his action to his words, and still keeping his revolver leveled at the professor, the outlaw pulled toward him a big cowskin bag, which, as he said truly, the scientist had kept with him night and day ever since he purchased it at a shop in Lima the morning of his arrival.

"Dawson," returned Professor Ditson, earnestly. "I give you my word as a gentleman that the treasure is now in the safe on the steamer which leaves the day after to-morrow, and I hold the receipt of the steamship company for it. Don't open that bag. There is nothing in it for you but—death."

"I'll see about that," muttered Scar Dawson. "Don't move," he warned, as the scientist started up from his bed. "I'll shoot if you make me."

Even as he spoke, he drew a knife from his belt and slit the leather side of the bag its whole length with a quick slash, and started to thrust in his hand.

As he did so he gave a yell of terror, for out from the opening suddenly appeared, wavering and hissing horribly, the ghastly head of the great bushmaster which the scientist had carried and cared for all the way from the Amazon basin. In another second, half its great length reared threateningly before the terrified outlaw. With one more yell, Dawson threw himself backward. There was a crash of broken glass, and by the time Will and Jud and Joe and their host, aroused by the noise, had reached the room, they found only Professor Ditson, coolly tying up the damaged bag, into which, by some means known only to himself, he had persuaded the bushmaster to return.

To-day, in the world-famous gem collection of Big Jim Donegan, in the place of honor, gleams and glows the great Emerald of the Incas. What he did for those who won the treasure for him, and how that same party of treasure-hunters traveled far to bring back to him that grim, beautiful, and historic stone of the Far East, the Red Diamond—well, that's still another story.